He studied her expression and his lips quirked upward in a sudden glimpse of a smile, and Poppy blinked at the reminder of the Nathan she'd once known, a smile she'd always treasured as a rare commodity even then.

And seeing it now tugged something in her gut, and again her gaze settled and lingered on the outline of his mouth, the tug intensifying. *Whoa! What?*

"So why are you here?"

Poppy blinked. *Jeez. Focus.* "Your business partner, Greg, recently got engaged to Petra Davros. I want to plan their wedding."

Nathan leaned back in his chair. "Then why are you sitting in my office, not Greg's?"

"Because without your support, I'm pretty sure he'll show me the door. But if you back me, maybe I stand a chance." She hesitated. "I know it's a big ask. I know you don't want me here. Know you don't want me in your life." The knowledge hurt, even after all these years. "But if you help me on this, I'll exit your life. No more birthday texts—I promise to leave you alone. Deal?"

Dear Reader,

When I started this story, all I knew was that I wanted to set it in Copenhagen, and I had a feeling that my hero and heroine had once known each other and the book would open with a reunion— one that neither of them actually wanted!

Turned out I was right. Poppy and Nathan really didn't want that reunion, and once they met, all either of them wanted was to keep that reunion as brief as possible. But events spiral, along with a growing attraction that they desperately try to ignore, and they end up in Copenhagen together.

I hope you enjoy reading what happens there and how Poppy and Nathan work out how to move forward from the past. There were times when I was worried they wouldn't!

Nina x

Wedding Planner's Deal with the CEO

Nina Milne

Recycling programs for this product may not exist in your area.

ISBN-13: 978-1-335-59637-6

Wedding Planner's Deal with the CEO

Copyright © 2023 by Nina Milne

For questions and comments about the quality of this book, please contact us at CustomerService@Harlequin.com.

Harlequin Enterprises ULC
22 Adelaide St. West, 41st Floor
Toronto, Ontario M5H 4E3, Canada
www.Harlequin.com

Printed in U.S.A.

Nina Milne has always dreamed of writing for Harlequin Romance—ever since she played libraries with her mother's stacks of Harlequin romances as a child. On her way to this dream, Nina acquired an English degree, a hero of her own, three gorgeous children and—somehow!— an accountancy qualification. She lives in Brighton and has filled her house with stacks of books—her very own *real* library.

Books by Nina Milne

Harlequin Romance

The Casseveti Inheritance

Italian Escape with the CEO
Whisked Away by the Italian Tycoon
The Secret Casseveti Baby

A Crown by Christmas

Their Christmas Royal Wedding

Whisked Away by Her Millionaire Boss
Baby on the Tycoon's Doorstep
Second Chance in Sri Lanka
Falling for His Stand-In Fiancée
Consequence of Their Dubai Night

Visit the Author Profile page
at Harlequin.com for more titles.

To all the wonderful people out there who dedicate their working lives to being carers.

Praise for
Nina Milne

CHAPTER ONE

POPPY WINCHESTER LOOKED down at her feet, seemingly stuck to the grey London pavement, and urged them forward. She tried to take courage from the designer high heels that were simple, stylish and bold, in a red that matched her nails and hair. The shoes were a perfect complement to the green business suit she was wearing, with its classic just-below-the-knee skirt, topped with a jade jacket with a black and white patterned overlay. A perfect combo of fashion and professionalism she had chosen to give herself confidence as well as convey it.

And damn it—it should be working. Projecting the right image through fashion was Poppy's forte, perhaps because style was in her blood. Her maternal grandmother had founded a fashion house that had thrived over the years and grown into a global brand. Carruci designs were known and acclaimed across the world.

A familiar dull hurt panged. Because style

might be in her blood but it wasn't in her future. She'd always believed that she would have a place in the Carruci empire. Until three years ago when, in the immediate aftermath of Poppy's disastrous break-up, her mother had dropped her bombshell. Told her that she would be leaving the Carruci empire solely to Poppy's half-siblings, the offspring of her happy, stable second marriage.

Poppy had been devastated by her mother's decision and the blunt confirmation of how Honor Carruci felt about her—that she wasn't family. Poppy had always known it, but this made it a final, irrevocable rejection.

She dug her nails into the palms of her hands. Now was not the time to dwell on the past and things she couldn't change. Now was the time to remember why she was standing here, in the heart of London's City. To save Star Weddings. The business that had been her best friend Bella's dream, a dream Bella had invited Poppy to be part of, giving her a thirty per cent stake in the company. But now the business was on the verge of ruin, the dream crumbling and Bella was devastated. Enough to confess to Poppy that she had fallen off the wagon after years of sobriety. Poppy hadn't hesitated—with Bella's consent she'd booked her friend into a rehab clinic and told her that she would deal with everything.

So here she was—enacting the only idea she could think of, an idea born of desperation. A plan that involved Nathan.

Hard to believe the prospect of seeing Nathan Larrimore could render her so nervous. Nathan who had once been her rock, her ally against a world that dealt too many surprises and shifts and twists. Her best friend from the age of seventeen when they'd met at college, her go-to person through the university years. But then, understandably, all that had changed when Nathan had met Alexis, the woman he'd fallen for, and in the past nine years their lives had veered in different directions, through tragedy and heartbreak. They were no longer allies; their once rock-solid friendship had cooled to a tepid, tenuous connection at best.

Poppy took a deep breath. Whatever the label, Nathan was her last hope. It was time to enter the imposing glass-fronted edifice in the heart of the City of London, which was flanked by the loom of skyscrapers of various shapes and sizes. Time to storm the building. Or at least stride womanfully in.

Of course, she could have tried to contact him to arrange a meeting, but if she'd done that he could have simply refused her request. So she'd decided that surprise and presence were her best chance of success and here she was.

She forced her red high heels into motion, took the last few steps and pushed through the revolving doors and into the lobby of the massive building, headed to the reception desk, strategically placed before the rows of automatic barriers that allowed entry to a selection of businesses, including Envii Enterprises, founded by Nathan, a design consultancy responsible for a vast array of environmentally friendly products, the latest being the Envii electric car, which had taken the country by storm.

She forced a bright smile to her face. 'Hi. My name is Poppy Winchester. I'm an old friend of Nathan Larrimore at Envii Enterprises. I was wondering if it would be possible to see him.'

The receptionist smiled. 'I'm afraid I'm not allowed to send people through without an appointment. Perhaps you should give him a call.'

'I was hoping to surprise him.'

'Unfortunately that won't be possible; I'm sure you understand—we have to think about security.'

Poppy held back a sigh; after all, she'd known it would come to this.

Pulling her phone out of her bag, she didn't give herself time to think, typed the text as quickly as she could.

* * *

Nathan Larrimore frowned as his phone pinged. The whole morning had been a string of distractions from what he was trying to do: tease out an idea that hovered in the forefront of his brain but that he couldn't quite grasp. Experience told him it would come, that all the research, all the knowledge would mingle and settle in his brain and eventually spark the idea he knew was there.

Nathan's lips set in an irritated line as he picked his phone up. And froze.

Hi Nathan. It's Poppy. I'm in the lobby. Can I come up?

A mixture of emotions rocked through him, memories of the past where he and Poppy had been friends, best friends, allies for ever, or so he had thought. But he'd been wrong because right after university their friendship had foundered, no, it had summarily collapsed when Poppy had withdrawn, exited for reasons he'd never understood, been barely present for all the years of his marriage. The pang of hurt reawakened as he looked down at her text…and then images flashed of their last meeting.

Four years ago, scant days after the death of his wife and he'd been raw with grief, a grief compounded and burdened by the weight of guilt. The knowledge that he'd let Alexis down, spent their marriage subsumed by work, hadn't listened, hadn't done enough. Had failed.

He'd found her diary, a diary he hadn't even known she'd kept, but as he'd read it his regrets and guilt had multiplied as he'd learnt more about Alexis than he'd ever known in life. Including her belief that Nathan had turned to her on the rebound from Poppy, that if Poppy hadn't vanished from his life he wouldn't have married Alexis. He could almost hear Alexis's voice reading the stark prose that outlined her loneliness and her longing that Nathan would be more present, the mortification at turning up to social events on her own constantly, her desire for a baby, her growing frustrations and her thoughts of divorce.

The words had confirmed that he deserved every ounce of guilt. The damning words there to stay, a tarnish on his very soul. Because he couldn't get away from the fact that marriage to him had made Alexis's tragically short life even more tragic. He wished he'd listened, been there, not missed birthdays or cancelled dates. He wished she had asked for a divorce, then at least she could perhaps have found happiness in the few years she'd had.

So when Poppy had arrived on his doorstep

after he had lost Alexis, Poppy whom he had seen only twice, briefly, in his four years of marriage, Nathan had been hit with a swirl of emotions.

His initial reaction, the one he'd instantly pushed down, had been one of happiness and that had wrenched the wound of grief and guilt further open.

So he'd asked her to go; it had seemed the very least he could do in honour of Alexis's memory, and since he'd steadfastly refused any further overtures so now all they did was exchange ever more anodyne birthday messages.

Until now.

He looked down at his phone.

Scrolled the messages over the past four years.

Happy Birthday, Nathan. I'm here if you need me.

Happy birthday, Nathan. Hope to hear from you soon.

Happy Birthday. Have a great day.

Happy birthday.

And now…now Poppy was downstairs. The question was why? What if she was ill? The idea sent panic through him…they might have lost touch but Poppy had once been the most important person in his life. If she was ill he'd never forgive himself for turning her away now and he carried enough regrets to last for ever.

But the thought of seeing her made him edgy. A ghost from the past and that was where he wanted her to stay. The past. In memory of Alexis, but also for himself. They'd been too close, she'd known him too well and that wasn't what he wanted, closeness, caring for others or having them care for him.

Enough. There was no question of rekindling closeness. That was over. He and Poppy had been friends years ago. Then *she* had decided to withdraw. And yet…if she was ill or in trouble…

Nathan drummed his fingers on the desk in uncharacteristic indecision, looked up at the ceiling for inspiration, sighed and started to type.

Poppy tried to ignore the curious look from the receptionist, stared down at her phone and wondered what was taking him so long. He'd read the damn thing, for Pete's sake. Ping. She looked down.

I'll send my PA down for you.

'He's sending his PA down,' she informed the receptionist as her tummy started to churn with a mix of anticipation and sheer nerves.

'That's great—I'm so sorry I couldn't let you up unannounced. I hope he's still surprised.'

'I think we can take that as a given.'

Before the rather puzzled receptionist could respond the lift door whooshed open and a young man strode across the marble floor.

'Poppy? I'm Ben, Nathan's PA. Let me show you up.'

She followed the dark-haired man back to the lift, hands clenched into fists, body taut with stretched nerves.

'Are you OK?' Ben asked. 'If you don't like lifts we can take the stairs.'

'I'm fine with lifts, but thank you.' She could hardly explain the hammer of her heart and her shallowness of breath were due to anxiety. Nathan was her last hope and she had no idea if he'd even hear her out. Assuming she could get the words out without choking on her pride. Coming cap in hand to a man who clearly wanted nothing to do with her was humiliating at best. But…not as humiliating as being dragged through a bankruptcy court.

Plus saving Star Weddings was worth a bit of humiliation. Though it was more than mortification—there were so many other emotions in the mix and it took all she had to not simply reach over and jab the button for the ground floor.

They stepped out of the lift and Ben led the way down the corridor, knocked on a door and popped his head round. 'I've got Poppy.'

A deep breath and she pushed the door open and entered the room, vaguely heard it click shut behind her as Ben left.

Poppy gulped, resisted the urge to run her hands down her skirt and stepped forward as Nathan rose to his feet. Her eyes searched his face, so familiar yet so different. Long gone now the over-long hair he'd sported at university, now his blond hair was cut into a sharp, short style. His face looked leaner, etched with tragedy and experience, the jut of his nose, the line of his jaw seemed sharper, more defined. He looked…harder, fitter, different, and for an insane moment her gaze lingered on him, mesmerised by his sheer presence, and her tummy clenched in a sudden twist of utterly unexpected desire.

What the…?

She braced herself, forced her senses to regroup. This was Nathan…her one-time friend who had summarily rejected that friendship at their last meeting. The reminder enough to summon a rush of hurt; a hurt she knew she had no right to feel. After all, he'd been ravaged by grief, reeling with pain after the death of his wife. Yet his rejection of her had stung; Nathan hadn't even let her over the threshold, his grey eyes arctic as he'd looked at her standing on the doorstep and she'd flinched at the near dislike she'd seen.

The memory etched into her brain. 'Just go, Poppy. Now. I don't care how far you've come from, or if you "hopped on the next plane". I don't need you. I don't want you here.' And with that he'd shut the door, left her staring blankly at the dark green painted wood.

She'd told herself he was in the first throes of grief, that he'd come round. But Nathan hadn't come round. She'd tried, messaged, called, left messages. In the end she'd taken the hint, given up.

Now she studied his grey eyes, wondered if he too was thinking back to the past and, if so, which bit. Eyes that once she'd been able to read like the proverbial book. Eyes that she'd seen hold laughter, pain, sadness… Which now held nothing but a cool neutrality. And she realised she had no idea what he was thinking. Other things had changed too—his body had filled out; he'd never be stocky or bulky but the word muscle came to mind—he looked like a man who could handle himself with confidence.

Shock raced through her alongside a frisson of something, a funny little tremor as her gaze settled on the breadth of his chest, the outline of his shoulders, ensconced in a suit her eye recognised as designer and tailored to fit him perfectly.

She needed to speak and yet for some reason her vocal cords felt taut and she realised that he too was silent as his grey eyes studied her and she saw something there—a flash, an arrest of shock and then the beginnings of a frown. She forced her brain to issue the command, finally managed, 'Hello, Nathan.'

'Poppy.'

'Thank you for agreeing to see me.'

'No problem. Sit down.' His eyes searched hers as she sank down onto the ergonomically designed chair, and despite the smoothness of his voice she thought she saw a flicker of anxiety in the grey depths, saw it in the clench of his jaw. 'Is there something wrong?'

Instinctively she knew what he was asking. 'I'm not ill,' she said instantly. 'That's not why I'm here.'

'Good.' The tension left those broad shoulders. 'So what can I do for you?'

Really? 'So you want to forgo small talk completely?' she asked.

A shrug and, 'Yes. I can't see the point in discussing the weather or revisiting the past.' A shadow clouded his eyes and she bit her lip. Of course Nathan didn't want to look back on Alexis's illness and death and for him the whole vista of the past must be overshadowed with that tragic event. 'I'd rather focus on the here and now.'

And again a silence threatened, as if the words had taken on a meaning of their own. Their gazes focused, met and she'd swear something shimmered in the air, a spark, a connection, an awareness... What the hell...? She shifted on the seat and now surprise flitted across his eyes before his mouth set in a hard line and her eyes lingered a fraction too long on the outline of those lips.

'I assume you want something, so please go ahead and explain.'

Welcome anger sparked at the curtness of his words even as she acknowledged the truth of them. Deep breath. She'd known this wouldn't be easy. But it was important, and she couldn't let emotion get in the way of her plan.

'You're right. I have come here to ask a favour.' She tucked a tendril of hair behind her ear, gave it a small tug to ground herself and met his gaze. 'I'm not sure if you know but I am a partner in a wedding business, Star Weddings. We started small and we built up a good reputation, and then we got offered the wedding of a lifetime.'

The expression on his face was unreadable, though he was probably wondering why he needed to know any of this.

'Della Mac's wedding,' she continued.

That at least got a response, a raised eyebrow, and he leant forward slightly.

'We were thrilled to get the chance.' Who wouldn't be? The diminutive singer had shot to fame and fortune with a series of hits that showed talent, flair and publicity savvy. 'So we put our all into it, one egg, one basket. We turned down other business and went for it. Della didn't want publicity about the wedding beforehand, didn't want interest in her relationship to take over the release of her latest album, but she promised us plenty of praise and publicity after the wedding itself. The wedding would have been lavish—a no-expense-spared event—and it would have put Star Weddings on the map. But then Della Mac and her fiancé split up at the last minute. No wedding. Worse, they both refused to pay.'

Nathan frowned. 'Take them to court. And surely you got them to pay as they went along.'

'It's a bit more complicated than that.' Poppy tried to keep her voice even; being dramatic wasn't going to gain Nathan's assent to her idea. Yet her remembered sense of horror when she'd realised the mess they were in threatened to shake her demeanour. Bella's stricken words of explanation.

'It's all my fault, Poppy. I messed up. I didn't push for payment when I should have. I was star-struck and then I was worried if I pushed she'd pull out and go somewhere else. So I told myself it would all be all right, that even if they didn't pay the publicity from the wedding would make up for it. That of course they'd pay because the money is peanuts to them. I know that was wrong, but I got caught up in this fantasy and I got so panicked when I thought about it that I didn't think and now...now we're verging on bankruptcy. God. I am so sorry.'

Poppy had stared at her friend, her usually sensible, financially astute, business-savvy friend. Seen the devastation on her face as she'd faced reality, watched the culmination of years and years of work dissolve because of one error of judgement. And Poppy knew how easy it was to misjudge a character—she'd misjudged Steve, believed what she'd wanted to believe. Even now her skin crawled at the memory of her own gullibility and humiliation.

So she was damned if she'd go through that sort of horror again—another media maelstrom—this time whilst being dragged through the bankruptcy courts, the failure of the 'non-heiress', the way her family would react. Confirmation that she was the failure they'd labelled her.

No way. That was why this had to work. The last throw of the dice.

'Complicated how?' Nathan asked and now he was all business, his grey eyes hard, and her gaze snagged on the uncompromising line of his mouth, the outline of his lips, the jut of his jaw.

'We messed up. We didn't handle the finances right. Now we're facing bankruptcy.' She wouldn't make excuses, accepted joint responsibility. She was a partner, she should have checked, should have noticed, should have acted differently on such a massive project.

He frowned, and now his eyebrows rose. 'Doesn't sound like the Poppy I knew, the one with the economics and business degree.'

'Well, the Poppy you knew has changed.' The Poppy who had done the degree because she'd wanted to bring something extra to the Carruci business. The Poppy who'd been foolish enough to believe her future in fashion was assured and bright. Well, that Poppy might be gone but this new one was determined to fight for what she had achieved. 'But this one wants to save her business.'

'So you're here to ask me to bail you out?'

'No!' She jutted her chin out determinedly and clenched her hands. 'Of course not. That is not why I am here.'

He studied her expression and his lips quirked upwards in a sudden glimpse of a smile and Poppy blinked at the reminder of the Nathan she'd once known, a smile she'd always treasured as a rare commodity even then. And seeing it now tugged something in her gut and *again* her gaze settled and lingered on the outline of his mouth and now the tug intensified. Whoa! What?

'So why are you here?'

Poppy blinked. *Jeez. Focus.* 'Your business partner, Greg, recently got engaged to Petra Davros.' Greg Breville, ex-racing driver, was now part of Envii Enterprises and Petra Davros a supermodel who had graced the pages of every fashion cover. 'I want to plan their wedding.'

Nathan leaned back in his chair. 'Then why are you sitting in my office, not Greg's?'

'Because without your support I'm pretty sure he'll show me the door. But if you back me, maybe I stand a chance.' She hesitated. 'I know it's a big ask. I know you don't want me here. Know you don't want me in your life.' The knowledge hurt, even after all these years. 'But if you help me on this, I'll exit your life— no more birthday texts, I promise to leave you alone. Deal?'

CHAPTER TWO

NO MORE POPPY in his life. The words descended with a gravity, a sense of finality that temporarily floored him. Which made no sense. After all, wasn't that exactly what he had wanted before Poppy had entered his office? To consign her to his past? And now here she was volunteering to be consigned. So why was he hesitating?

Especially as seeing Poppy had brought up a swirl of emotions: happiness, guilt, and an instinctive desire to help her, have her back, go and force Della Mac and her fiancé to cough up their dues. It felt as though the world had extra colour, but Poppy had always done that to him; her zest for life, her attitude, the vividity of her presence had always made him feel that extra edge of alive.

But with that edge came a sense of responsibility, an involvement, feelings. And he didn't want any of those things. Didn't want Poppy back in his life—that would be a true betrayal of Alexis's memory and what he owed her.

Yet reluctance lingered as he studied her, unable to help himself. The auburn hair, which shone, shimmered threads of red in the sunlight that flickered through his office windows. The green eyes, a sea of emotions, each one a different glint of green, a chin that spoke of resolution, the nose retroussé and her mouth, lips a perfect curve, lips that snagged his gaze, made him linger on their shape, their... What the hell was he doing?

Whoa. Discomfort rocked him back in his seat as he acknowledged what he had tried to ignore ever since she'd entered the room. He'd set eyes on her and everything had gone into overdrive as he'd taken her in. Seen how she'd put herself together, the businesslike hairstyle, the red and green suit that mixed professional with flair. He realised she still used clothes as armour, utilised them to project whatever she wanted to project. That sense of familiarity and then...*kazoom*! Something had happened, a jolt, an awareness of something shocking in its newness, its sheer unexpectedness.

Something even now he didn't want to put a name to. But, whatever it was, it was yet another reason to take the deal. He could not let Poppy back into his life; long ago she had chosen to make her exit and now it was time to make that permanent.

'Deal,' he said and told himself he imagined the flicker of hurt in her eyes. 'Provided you convince me that you can do the job. I won't recommend you unless I believe you can do it. And even if I do, I'm not sure they will agree. Greg and I are partners—that's no reason for them to let me choose their wedding planner.'

'I get that. But you must have some influence. You and Greg are friends as well.'

'Yes.' They were. They'd become friends during Greg's glory years but then at the apex of his career he'd crashed, smashed his knee up and that had been the end—an end he'd struggled to come to terms with.

Missing the adrenalin high of racing, Greg had turned to the casinos, decided high-stakes gambling was the answer. Nathan knew all too well through bitter personal experience where gambling addiction landed you—in his father's case it had been prison. So one day he'd marched into the casino, forced his friend to leave and given him a choice. Quit gambling and come into business with him. A month later Greg had been on board and a year later the Envii range of electric cars had been launched to fanfare and success. So, yes, Greg was a friend. 'But I am pretty sure he is leaving the wedding decisions to Petra.'

'But it won't hurt to have Greg's support and all I need is a chance to convince Petra. Once I convince you. And I can. They will get an amazing wedding. Bella and I are good at what we do. I've brought a portfolio of previous weddings we've organised, all magical, all unique and completely tailor-made to what the clients wanted.' She paused as she studied his face. 'What? You're looking...surprised.'

Another emotion to go alongside curiosity. 'I suppose I am. I would never have imagined you'd sound so passionate about being a wedding planner.' For a start, he'd always believed Poppy's heart lay with fashion. 'And I didn't think you believed in happy ever after.' And who could blame her? Her father was a serial womaniser who went through wives like others went through tissues. And Poppy had hated it, the chaos, the ever-changing women, most of whom had had little time for her.

She shrugged now, slim shoulders lifted in a characteristic motion that was, oh, so familiar, and as he watched her, saw the small twist of her lips, there it was again, the frisson, the tug of desire. He closed his eyes, warded off panic. Desire—he'd named it now, admitted it.

'I don't believe in a happy ever after for myself. Tried that and it didn't work.' Pain crossed her face and he recalled the headlines of three years ago, detailing an acrimonious break-up, headlines he'd skimmed over. Had refused to be interested, couldn't, because his days of being able to care, be a friend, were gone. It would have been disloyal to Alexis's memory to rush to help Poppy when he hadn't been there for his own wife.

'But just because it didn't work for me doesn't mean it won't work for other people. And even if it doesn't work out, everyone deserves a wedding day to remember, the day when they believed it could happen, when they decided to commit to each other. Whatever the future holds.' She paused and bit her lip. 'I'm sorry, Nathan. That was insensitive of me. I didn't mean to bring back bad memories for you.'

'That's OK. You're right. Alexis loved our wedding day—she truly did.' He remembered how she had been bubbling with happiness and how he too had felt a deep contentment. Was sure that the future would be solid, that he would never follow in his father's footsteps, end up destroying his marriage, a gambling addict who threw away everything and ended up in prison. The whole future had been full of promise. How wrong he'd been. But the wedding itself had been exactly as Alexis had wanted.

'OK. You've convinced me you're committed. But what about finance? If you go under halfway through organising the wedding that's hardly fair.'

'I would never risk that. So I've put together a plan. As of now we have some space until the majority of the invoices are due. If I can win Petra and Greg's business, on the basis of our past performance I will be able to negotiate a loan because the bank will see that we are a going concern. I will make absolutely sure this wedding is financially viable.'

'Because this time you'll be in charge of finance rather than Bella.' The statement was made from instinct. He knew, however much Poppy had changed, she wouldn't have let the finances get 'complicated', would not have been responsible for her business heading to the bankruptcy courts.

'Yes, or we'll do it togeth—' She broke off and glared at him. 'That was low, Larrimore. Bella and I are partners; I take joint responsibility for the decisions.'

Larrimore. It was what she'd called him when they'd first met, two misfitting seventeen-year-olds at a sixth-form college. He the son of a criminal and a drunk, she the heiress to not one but two separate business empires.

'Fair enough, but if I am going to recommend you I want you to be in charge of the money. And I want the truth. I won't sell a dud to Greg and Petra.'

'Fine. Bella was in charge of the finance. I am more the junior partner in the business and that has been fine by me. This is Bella's dream business—she has always believed in the fairy tale, and always wanted to do this. And usually she does everything right, we have built up slowly, had money in the bank, but with this wedding, she misjudged and made a mistake. It won't happen again. And I can show you the costed-out business plan of how we will go forward.' She reached into the slimline briefcase she carried and pulled out a file, handed it across the desk.

He reached out to take it, took an absurd level of care to grasp the edge of the plastic, to make sure he had absolutely no physical contact with her, practically snatched the folder.

She reached back down and pulled out another file. 'I also brought details of a couple of the weddings we organised; I put some photos into an album, but I've also brought the costings for each. To demonstrate that we do have some financial grasp.' The words were said with a mixture of tartness and rue.

She placed the albums on the desk and he

reached over and pulled them towards him, opened the top one and studied the pictures.

'That was one of the first weddings we did two years ago, it was relatively high profile, Lady Harriet Stevens, and it was such fun. She wanted something different and adventurous so she and the groom literally hiked up a mountain together and we held the ceremony at the top. That's why…' She reached over to point at a particular photo, and inadvertently her hand touched his. He felt his hand jump upwards as if scorched, and her voice jerked to a falter as she tugged her own away.

Nathan inhaled deeply. He had to get a grip—electric shocks, et cetera, et cetera, didn't exist. It was evidently static, or something of the sort. He was a scientist and an engineer, for heaven's sake. 'Go on,' he said.

'Yes…um…' She pointed again. 'That's why I found that dress and then had it altered, into a sort of Victorian walking dress style but with added practicality and wedding glamour. And I was particularly happy with the hiking boots—I gave them a wedding makeover. And we had a pair of designer high heels for when she got to the top.'

'The day was obviously a success,' he said as he continued to turn the pages, and he meant it. The pictures clearly showed the spirit of the wedding, a sense of adventure, the joy and exhilaration of the couple apparent.

'The other one is a more conventional wedding. I wanted to demonstrate that we know that the most important thing is what the couple want and every wedding is unique and special and needs to be something a couple can look back on, and see that their marriage got off to a happy, wonderful start. I can give that to Greg and Petra. Do you believe me?'

'Yes.' Nathan could feel himself being swept up in her belief, hated to rain on her parade, but... 'But I can't guarantee they will.'

'All I ask for is a chance. Back my bid and help me get in front of them so I can pitch. And regardless of how it goes I'll be out of your life.'

'I'll do my best.'

'Thank you. Really, Nathan, I mean it.' She rose to her feet, a lithe, graceful movement, tucked a tendril of deep red hair behind her ear and smiled, and something caught in his chest, caused him to reach out to grab the edge of his desk as he too stood. 'I'm not sure what to do,' Poppy said softly. 'Do we shake hands or hug or...how do we say goodbye?'

'I...' Proximity was not a good idea. Ridiculous. This was Poppy. Poppy whom he'd spent his late teenage and early twenties in very close proximity to, stayed up late drinking and talking with, gone on holiday with… But back then he'd never felt this strange sense of breathlessness.

Nathan blinked fiercely. *Come on, man, prove to yourself how ridiculous this is.* This was goodbye to a part of his past, perhaps that explained the odd sensation, but he was damned if he'd show it. He walked round the desk and said, 'A hug will be fine.'

Even as the words dropped he knew they were sheer bravado—he didn't do hugs and instinct told him this was a bad idea. But too late.

Poppy looked up at him and there was that breathlessness again as he took in her features—the wide-open green eyes, fringed by impossibly long lashes, eyes that held a wealth of emotion, emerald sparkles of warmth, regret and an elusive something else. Her sleek red hair, which he'd used to ruffle to annoy her, slanted cheekbones and a straight, almost aquiline nose dusted with the faintest of freckles.

He realised that he had stepped back, could feel the edge of his desk against the backs of his thighs, heard the catch of her breath now. His brain tried to cut through, work out what the hell was going on. He looked at her again and realised that he wanted to kiss her.

Hell.

He forced himself to break eye contact, terrified she'd see the desire, and forced himself to step forward, forced himself to smile, knew it was more grimace. Braced himself as Poppy too stepped forward, put her arms around him in a quick, awkward gesture.

He could smell her perfume, a light vanilla essence. Her hair tickled his nose as he managed to raise his hands to pat her back, her body too close to his, the nearness sending unwanted sensations through him, and they both leapt backwards. She gave a fleeting look up at him and in that instant he knew she'd felt it too, and was as shocked as him.

'Right. Thank you again. I'll wait to hear from you. Text if that's easier. I will be completely flexible. Happy to meet Petra and Greg wherever they want. Right…um…it was good to see you even if I won't be seeing you again. OK. Bye.'

With that, she was gone, the door clicking shut behind her.

Poppy placed her mobile phone on the table in the small London flat she rented—a far cry from the massive house she'd shared with Steve. That house had been 'worthy' of the supposed heiress to two fashion empires and she'd accepted the house as a gift from her father. Accepted it not because she'd loved the house, but because she'd loved Steve. Steve had wanted the house and all the trappings of wealth and she'd wanted whatever Steve wanted.

But she couldn't blame only Steve; Poppy had been thrilled that her dad liked Steve, that her relationship had brought her into the fold. And so she'd gone along with all that entailed, accepted an allowance, embraced the lavish lifestyle as Steve had wanted.

What a fool she'd been, gullible, naïve…in love. Look where that had got her…the humiliation of Steve's affairs, the realisation that history was repeating itself before her very eyes, that she'd been deluded enough to fall for a man who was a carbon copy of her own womanising, cheating father. No wonder they got on so well. Steve was like the son her father had never had, a fact her half-brother, Michael, Jonathan Winchester's actual son, was all too aware of. And her refusal to listen to Michael, who had warned her about Steve, had tarnished her relationship with her half-brother.

But that was the past…and she would not think of it now. Now she was happy in this small rented flat that she'd made her own, a flat paid for by her own money, from a business she was partner in, a business that was nothing to do with either parent. And nothing to do with fashion. Because when she'd broken up with Steve, when her dad had taken Steve's side, she'd decided 'enough'. She was going to cut herself off from her family—not in a dramatic way, but she needed to make her own life. A fresh clean start, away from the past. And now here she was embroiled in a different bit of her past.

Nathan.

She'd spent the past hours endeavouring not to think about Nathan, not wanting to face the stark reality of their meeting.

Nathan didn't want her in his life. At all. Full stop.

That had hurt—way, way more than she'd anticipated.

But that wasn't what she was shying away from—she was trying to block out the mad idea that there had been a shimmer of attraction. She'd wanted to kiss him, kiss Nathan, and for a split second she'd swear that desire had been reciprocal. She closed her eyes and opened them again. It was probably, *had to be*, a figment of her imagination or a reaction to seeing him after all these years, or stress, or the fact she hadn't dated in a long time and Nathan was an attractive man so her hormones had just got a little mixed up.

All that mattered was if he could secure her a meeting with Petra and Greg.

Poppy picked up her phone for the millionth time, nearly dropped it when it rang.

Hurriedly she answered it.

'Nathan?'

'Poppy. I spoke to Greg and Petra.' Her fingers tightened round the phone as she heard the exasperation in his voice. 'They aren't sure at all. I persuaded them to consider the idea, but they want us both to meet with them to discuss it.'

Emotions swirled inside her: relief that there was a chance she could pull this off, and panic that Nathan was still part of the scenario. 'Why do they want you there as well?'

'Petra wants me to "put my money where my mouth is"—she wants to make sure my backing you is legit.'

Which was fair enough. This was Petra's wedding. Nathan was asking her to take a gamble and use someone he recommended, someone Petra had never even known was part of Nathan's life.

'I get that, but it's not part of our agreement. Will you do it?'

'Yes. It's one more meeting, and it would look odd to refuse. They want to meet tomorrow evening.'

'That's fine.' She hesitated, hated to ask, but, hell, she'd already swallowed pride and inclination by reaching out to Nathan in the first place. 'Would you mind…?'

'Meeting you beforehand so I can go through exactly what they said and what I said so you have all the information possible before tomorrow?'

'Yes. I know it's a big ask.'

'It's also a sensible one. I understand you want to maximise your chances. I've got meetings all day tomorrow, but if you want we could meet up now.' And get it over with… He didn't say the words but she sensed them. 'Somewhere discreet—we don't want any publicity.'

'Agreed.'

Nathan Larrimore hadn't been spotted with a woman since Alexis's death four years ago. So being caught on camera together could only lead to speculation of a kind neither of them wanted.

'Why don't we meet at Bella's flat? She's away at the moment.'

'Sure. Send me the address. I'll leave now.'

CHAPTER THREE

NATHAN APPROACHED THE London address Poppy had given him, sure that no one had followed him or shown any interest in his movements. He wished he were back at home, working, finalising the buy-out of his new venture, trying to work out that elusive formula that he couldn't quite see. Yet.

Only…that wish wasn't completely true— there was a very tiny part of him that *wanted* to see Poppy and that was *exasperating*.

The whole situation was. The conversation with Greg and Petra had not gone as he had expected or wanted and now…well, now he was an unwilling broker to a deal he'd hoped to have nothing more to do with.

This was what happened when you got involved.

Sometimes involvement was compulsory— Nathan knew that and he would never sidestep his responsibilities. That wasn't his way—it never had been. Ever since a childhood where he'd had to pick up the pieces when his father had toppled from his pedestal. A man who Nathan had adored, looked up to, admired, had turned out to have feet of clay and when he'd fallen from his pedestal the fall had shattered Nathan's life.

Maurice Larrimore had been an outward success, high up in the banking world, wife, son, massive house, nice car, lavish lifestyle. But he'd also been a secret gambler and that addiction had cost him everything. He'd embezzled funds to pay his gambling debts, been caught and sent to prison. Leaving his wife and Nathan with nothing, the rug pulled from under their feet.

Nathan's mother had collapsed, turned to alcohol as a crutch and Nathan's life had turned upside down. He'd stepped up as best he could, aged thirteen, he'd closed down emotion, the only way he knew to come to terms with the fact his father had been a fraud. That and to vow to make up for it, to be different. To be a true success, and look after his mum, fix everything, give her back the lifestyle she'd lost. So he'd blocked out the bullying at school, made worse by his mother's drunken appearances at sports day and events or even the school gates.

And he had become a success. Successful

business, enough money to give his mother back the lifestyle she'd lost and then some, a marriage where he'd provided the real thing. A house they'd owned, a business built on solid foundations… He'd believed he'd made it, surpassed his father. How very wrong he'd been.

His mother still drank, and his marriage had floundered and he'd been as guilty as his father—been a failure of a husband. Worse in that at least his father had made his mother happy for fifteen years. Whereas Nathan had messed the whole thing up. Irrevocably.

So no more involvement, no more responsibility other than to his business.

And he'd stuck to that for four years until… Poppy had turned up and here he was *involved*.

Chill, Nathan. This was an overreaction. A couple of days and he was done, could get back to his normal life. Focus on his new project— the ideas whizzing and fizzing around his head. Hopefully all those strands were busy figuring out how to fit together.

On that heartening thought he stepped forward and rang the buzzer, pushed the communal door open when it buzzed and stepped into the hallway as Poppy opened the front door to the ground-floor flat.

And wham. There it was, yet another overreaction. A jolt, a picking up of where he'd left off—a sense of unmistakable visceral desire that caught him hard in the solar plexus. Sent heat through his veins and a rush of panic. This was Poppy—the idea of being attracted to Poppy was impossible. And yet…how else to explain these feelings as he absorbed her appearance, clocked the shapeless jumper that somehow only served to remind him of the shape beneath it, the long slim legs encased in jeans? He gulped, tried to cover it with a cough.

He needed to pull this together, instead of standing here like a goop, goggling at her. Even if she were doing the same: standing in the doorway, staring at him with a look of shock in her green eyes. Shock because she could read his thoughts or shock because those feelings were reciprocated?

He didn't know and he didn't want to find out. Because this was all a mistaken hormonal reaction, a generic one—after all, Poppy was universally recognised to be a beautiful woman and now he was no longer seeing her through the lens of close friendship his libido had the wrong end of the stick.

Schooling his features, he stepped forward. 'Poppy, I'm sorry about this.' *Oh, God.* What if she thought he was apologising for staring at her? 'I mean, the meeting including me. It wasn't my idea.'

'I know that. I'm sorry you're still involved.' The words sounded forced, as if she was as shaken as he was.

'Well, now that I'm here let's work out how we are going to play this.' The pronoun kicked into him—he and Poppy hadn't been a 'we' for a long time.

'Tell me exactly what Petra said.' Poppy led the way into a comfortable lounge-diner and headed to a small round table, sat on a wooden chair and waited for him to sit opposite her.

'Sorry.' Their knees bumped under the table and he pushed the chair back in a too jerky movement, told himself to stop behaving like an adolescent. Hell, he hadn't been like this when he was an adolescent.

'No problem.' She raised a hand and tangled a tendril of hair round her finger, her voice surely ever so slightly breathless. A tug on her hair and she took a deep breath. 'Right. Go ahead.'

'So at first Petra refused point-blank—said she wanted the best and she had no need to take a risk on someone who was on the verge of going out of business, plus she didn't like being tainted with failure.'

'Ouch. And then?'

'I suggested she look at it from a different angle. As positive publicity for her—Petra is branching out into a fashion business and one of the problems she is having is switching her model persona, which is a bit diva-like, to a more businesslike one.'

'And that worked?'

'Not at first, as she pointed out that it was hardly a good decision as a businesswoman to use someone whose business was tanking.'

To his surprise Poppy laughed. 'I can't really argue with that.'

'Well, I did,' he said. 'I pointed out, as a business decision, getting a dream wedding at a discounted cost was sensible, that it wasn't really a risk as it had a guaranteed return.'

'You said that? A guaranteed return?'

'Yes, I did.' He shrugged. 'Earlier when you spoke about the business, when you showed me those portfolios, what you'd done, I could hear the passion in your voice, how much this means to you, but also what you achieved. Those weddings… You made people happy—whatever happened to those people afterwards, on the day you created happiness. And doing so was important to you. That matters.'

And it did.

'I also told Petra that you admitted you made a mistake, but you want to save your business and you don't want the press to get hold of this, an heiress going through the bankruptcy court. They'd vilify you because of your name. That touched a chord with her. And with Greg. They've both had their share of bad press, experienced being kicked when they were down.'

Poppy blinked and to his surprise he saw a tear glint in the green of her eyes, rendering them an even more intense emerald. She reached out, covered his arm and the touch of her slender fingers seemed to burn through the cotton of his shirt. 'Thank you. You didn't have to do all that. All you promised was to ask them to see me; you didn't agree to fight my corner. I… I didn't think you'd do that any more.'

He glanced down at her hand, knew her touch shouldn't be affecting him, and then she raised her hand and gently touched his cheek and now he froze and so did she as she stared at him wide-eyed, before dropping her hand as though she'd been scorched.

'So thank you,' she said briskly. 'Did Petra say anything else?'

'Not really, though she did ask about your style and how you handle yourself—I imagine she is thinking that, if she does go ahead, she wants to know you'll do the publicity side successfully.'

'What did you say?'

'I said style is your thing…that if you hadn't

found your vocation as a wedding planner you'd easily get a job in a fashion house.'

He frowned as he saw her try to hide an obvious wince, the flash of hurt in her green eyes, and wondered at it. Again. Back in the day he'd always believed Poppy was destined to be a massive success in the fashion world. He'd catch her at odd moments sketching ideas, or she'd somehow pull together the most incredible outfit from what to him looked like a mismatched assortment of clothes. A corner of every place she'd lived was designated for a sewing machine where she'd try things out.

But it seemed as if Poppy had found a different vocation.

'Anything else?'

'She did ask about us. Our friendship and why I'd never mentioned you.' He could hear how reluctant the words sounded, but knew Poppy had a right to know everything that was said. 'I think she thought I may be making it up.'

'Our friendship? Why would you make it up?'

'If I had a different reason for recommending you.' He felt as though his shirt collar were too tight. Awkwardness sparkled in the air. 'Like… we were dating.'

'Dating. You and me?' Poppy laughed but

it felt to Nathan as if that laugh was a touch forced. 'I hope you explained how ridiculous that is.'

'Of course.' The words sounded way too loud and he'd swear the temperature had gone up in the room. 'I explained about being friends at school and university, said I could probably find an old photograph.' He glanced down as his phone buzzed, relieved at the distraction. 'That's Petra now. Confirming tomorrow. Seven-thirty at their house.'

'Great. I'll be there.'

'Just you or is Bella going to be part of this?'

'Just me. Bella's gone away for a few days, to get her head together.'

'But surely you could contact her—I mean, she must want to be part of this.'

Poppy bristled. 'I can handle this myself. Of course, if it all works out then Bella will be in charge but for now it's all still a bit of a long shot. So at this stage it's me on my own.'

He looked at her, sensed she was holding back, but even if she was she was clearly quite capable of making the pitch to Petra and Greg and the reasons for it were nothing to do with him.

'I'll pick you up.' He shrugged. 'That's what a friend would do.'

'OK. Thank you. Pick me up from here. That will be more discreet.'

And here was that moment of awkward again, the how to say goodbye, as he rose and backed away towards the door, tripped over a small table. 'Right. I'll see you tomorrow, then.'

Twenty-four hours later and Poppy stared at her reflection in Bella's full-length mirror hoping she'd got it right. Jumped as the doorbell buzzed, took a deep breath then grabbed her briefcase and headed for the door. As she exited through the communal door she gulped, wishing that Nathan didn't have this effect on her.

The muscle-clenching dip and pitch of her tummy, the pulse acceleration, all caused by what? The answers reeled. The spike of his blond hair, the swell of muscle under the long-sleeved top, the breadth of his shoulders, the look of arrest in his grey eyes.

'Hey.'

'Hey.' She tried to think of something, anything, to say, but her brain had scrambled. Because seeing him standing in the dusk, silhouetted by the London street lamps, she wanted to loop her arms around his neck and kiss him. A clear indication that there was something seriously wrong with her, some sort of acute miscommunication going on with her nerves, synapses, brains…something. *Talk, for heaven's sake.*

'So what do you think? Do I pass muster?' She gestured downwards to indicate her outfit. 'I'm hoping the top hints at traditional bridal, off white with a bit of floral embroidery, whilst the shoes are more of a fun fashion statement, because weddings should be fun.'

He nodded as he looked down at the chunky platform sandals, probably wondering why she was telling him any of this, but she couldn't seem to stop herself. 'Then my hair is supposed to combine fashion, professional and again a bit of bridal.' She'd caught her red waves up in a gold hair clip with a few artfully arranged tendrils framing her face. 'So hopefully it gives the right signals. Subtly.'

She looked at his expression and frowned— he looked exasperated, his lips set in a grim line.

'Have I got it wrong? Is there something in this outfit that gives the wrong impression, or that Petra will dislike?'

'No. No, truly, you look…' he hesitated '…fine. Petra will appreciate your sense of style.'

Fine? Poppy told herself it didn't matter what Nathan thought, and yet it did. Which was mortifying in itself. 'Even if you don't.' Her voice was flat and she shook her head. 'Sorry. There is no reason for you to appreciate my style. I'm nervous and you looked distinctly disapproving.'

'Not of you.'

Poppy frowned. Then of whom? Petra? Himself? She opened her mouth to ask but before she could he continued to speak.

'Not of anyone. I'm not disapproving, at all. I was just thinking it's a bit silly to be standing here, in case we're spotted.'

'Good point.' Though Poppy was convinced that wasn't what he had meant at all, but she couldn't be sure, could no longer read Nathan as she had once been able to. They started walking to the car and she climbed into the gleaming silver Envii.

'Is it strange, driving a car you designed yourself?'

'Not strange, more analytical. Every time I drive one I feel pride, but it also sparks my mind to think of ways to improve it.'

'And have you?'

'Greg and I are working on a more budget-friendly Envii car.'

She glanced at him, 'But I'm betting you have another project in mind that is nothing to do with cars.'

That got his attention; he kept his eyes on the road but she could see the rise of his eyebrows.

'Actually, yes, I am working on something

new. I'm buying out a vegan food company and I'm working on a new way to make plant-based "steak".' He drew to a halt at a traffic light and now he turned his head. 'OK. I'll bite. How did you know?'

'Lucky guess. You always liked having a lot of ideas on the go and Envii cars have been around for a few years now, I figured you'd be ready to turn that brain of yours to something new.'

'Well, you're right there. But we shouldn't be talking about me. Are there any last-minute points you want to run over before we get to Petra and Greg?'

Poppy shook her head. 'I haven't prepared a pitch as such. All I can do is answer their questions and hope I can convince them to use me. I've gone through various scenarios and tried to anticipate what they may ask.' Nerves started to ripple and she closed her eyes; remembered what was at stake.

'Right. We're here,' Nathan said and in minutes he had driven through an imposing set of gates in the celebrity-strewn, posh part of London, and parked on the sweeping courtyard. He turned to face her, the glow of the outside lights glinting in his blond hair. 'You OK?'

'There's so much riding on this. Not just for me but for Bella. She took a chance on me, let me share her dream, and I want to repay the favour.'

He reached out and covered her hand. 'You've got this.'

And there it was again, the shimmer, the jolt of awareness as they both looked down at their hands, before he hurriedly removed his and moved to open the car door.

As they walked towards the front door Poppy resisted the urge to stare down at her fingers. What was going on? Didn't matter. She had to focus on business now, push aside the fact that her hand still tingled from his touch, put aside the ridiculous burgeoning desire that Nathan was provoking. Ridiculous didn't begin to cover it and no way would she let it adversely affect this chance to save Star Weddings.

The door opened to reveal a tall dark-haired man, easily recognisable as Greg Breville. 'Nathan.' The men exchanged some complicated handshake and then Greg turned to smile at Poppy. 'And you must be Poppy Winchester. Pleased to meet you. Come through. Petra's in the lounge.'

Minutes later Poppy smiled as Petra Davros approached. In person Petra was every bit as beautiful as her images. Blonde, ice cool, blue-eyed, tall and stunning.

She stepped forward, hand outstretched.

'Poppy Winchester.' She met Petra's gaze full on, had no problem with the assessment in the blonde woman's eyes. 'Thanks for agreeing to see me.'

'Nathan spoke highly of you.' The model's blue eyes glanced from Poppy to Nathan.

'I'm glad and now I'm here to hopefully prove him right.'

'I've also done some research, made some calls. I know you have planned some amazing weddings. Yet Nathan tells me you need my help because you're on the verge of bankruptcy.'

'Yes.' What else could she say? There were no excuses.

'Normally I wouldn't even consider using you with or without Nathan's endorsement, but...' now she turned to look at Greg, and Poppy could see the love in her eyes '...Greg wants to give you a chance.'

The dark-haired man walked over to his fiancée and looped his arm round her shoulder. 'There have been a few fiascos in my life and without the second chances I've received I wouldn't be where I am today. I might not even be alive.'

'But on the other hand, this is my wedding we're talking about.' Petra stated matter-of-factly. 'It's...'

'Important,' Poppy finished for her. 'I know and I understand that. I also know that you would be taking a leap of faith.'

'And an unnecessary risk.'

'A risk with a guaranteed return,' Nathan said.

'Perhaps, but those are words. Also I want planning my wedding to be fun, not stressful, and if I am stressed throughout the whole process because I think you may go under, or may skimp on something or overcharge me, then...'

'Your wedding won't be a thing of joy,' Poppy said. 'I understand. If there is no trust then this can't work.' She tried to keep the disappointment from her voice even as she wondered if it was something she'd done or said, the way she looked.

Petra shook her head. 'I'm sorry. I know you must feel as though I wasted your time. I honestly thought this was a viable possibility, but now when it comes to the crunch I don't think it can work. Nathan hasn't seen you for years—he can't really vouch for you.' She looked up at Greg. 'I'm sorry. I know you wanted to do this.'

'It's OK,' Poppy broke in. 'Honestly. You do not need to apologise. I truly do understand. If using me as a wedding planner is going to take away from the whole wedding experience for you, then you shouldn't do it.'

Poppy focused on keeping her expression professional, cool, as if this didn't matter, hadn't been her last roll of the dice. She'd tried, but she couldn't make Petra want to use her. Worse, she could see the other woman's point of view.

Then Nathan stepped forward. 'I've got a suggestion,' he said.

CHAPTER FOUR

HE HAD? Poppy turned to look at him, as last-minute hope unfurled.

'Go ahead,' Petra said.

There was a moment of silence and Poppy wondered if Nathan regretted his intervention, though he gave no sign of it. Then, 'You're right—I haven't seen Poppy for a while, and so maybe I can't guarantee she will get it right. But I do *believe* she will.' He gestured to Poppy. 'Tell Petra how you work, the first thing you do when you accept an assignment.'

Poppy stepped forward. 'I need a meeting with you and Greg. You give me some ideas about what you want, the absolutes that you need, locations, guest numbers, types of venue and then I go away and come up with a detailed proposal or a number of proposals depending on how solid your ideas are. Then we sit down together and finalise the plan.'

Nathan nodded. 'So this is what I suggest.

Let Poppy come up with the proposal, but to take away your worries that she won't get it right I'll be part of putting the proposal together, that way I can give my input as your friend but I will also make sure all the costing, pricing et cetera is fair and accurate. Then once you have the proposal you decide from there. But I will vouch for the proposal.'

Poppy glanced across at Nathan's eyes and saw the glint of shock in their grey depths. Yup. Looked as if he'd surprised himself as much as he'd surprised her.

Petra took a deep breath, glanced up at her fiancé and they had some sort of silent communication. 'That sounds fair.' She looked from one to the other. 'If you're good with that, Poppy?'

Was she? Of course she was—Nathan had pulled a proverbial rabbit out of the hat and now she had a chance. Star Weddings had a chance. 'More than good. I completely understand your reservations and I'm happy to work with Nathan. Let me know when you'd like to discuss ideas and we can get started.'

'That's easy. Why not now? It won't really take very long. Because I haven't got any ideas. All I know is that I'd like it to be in Copenhagen.'

'That's a good start. I've never been there but—'

'Oh, neither have I,' Petra said cheerfully.

'But it's where my parents met.' Sadness flitted across her face. 'They died in a car crash when I was pretty young, but I'll always remember them telling the story of how they met in Copenhagen. That it was fate, they were both passing through and they met in a bar. And kaboom. So I'd like to get married there, a small wedding and then a week or so later a big party back in England.'

'Any themes or ideas, adventurous, scenic...'

'Perhaps you could check out the different options?' Petra gave a sudden smile. 'I'm not trying to be difficult. And I'll happily pay you a consulting fee. I've just never got married before and to be honest I never thought I would.' She looked up at Greg and the love in her eyes caught Poppy, the vulnerability there so at odds with Petra's aura. 'Greg caught me by surprise, but the problem is I know I want to get married but my mind blanks when I think about the how. So I can't tell you what I want.'

'Then my job is to help you figure that out.' She thought for a moment. 'And the best way I can do that is to go to Copenhagen, check out all the options in person so I can give you a real idea of your choices.'

'That sounds like a good plan.' Greg turned to Nathan. 'And I can hold the fort at work—at least all the car-related things.'

Huh? Poppy opened her mouth to intercede, took a beat to calm her breathing so that she could speak without the shrill tone of panic. This whole thing was unravelling and now, before she could speak, Petra gave the whole fabric another tug. 'I'd love it if you both went. That way Nathan is on hand to see everything and give his input.'

'So are we agreed? What do you reckon, mate?' Greg asked and all eyes turned to Nathan.

What did he reckon? He reckoned he must have lost the plot, the dictionary, the whole damn playbook. Otherwise he wouldn't have come up with his suggestion to help in the first place. It had been as though an alien Nathan had taken over his brain and instructed his vocal cords. And look where that had got him—the domino effect continued and now he was on the verge of his non-involvement policy being blown up to smithereens. Yet this was all his own fault; he couldn't even blame Poppy. Though with hindsight when her text had arrived he should have locked the door and hidden under his desk.

But there must be something he could do—because going to Copenhagen with Poppy was a terrible idea. 'It's a great idea, but I'm not sure it's really necessary,' he said. 'I am confident Poppy can do this without me being physically present.'

'Absolutely.' Poppy's voice was a welcome back-up, and he could only hope that only he could hear the underlay of panic that lined the well-modulated words. 'I'm more than happy to go to Copenhagen on my own—I'm sure Nathan and Greg have tonnes on at work and it's such short notice. And I can check in with him every day, do video calls and—'

'Actually Nathan's got a relatively light schedule this week,' Greg said cheerfully and for a moment Nathan wanted to kick his business partner, friend or no friend. 'Didn't you even say you should get away from the office so you can think about the new product? This is the perfect solution.'

'I think I'd prefer it if you were actually there, Nathan. It's not only about trust—I'd like to know Greg is represented. This is his wedding too.' He recognised the nuance of Petra's tone, used it himself in business often enough, a diplomatic way of framing an absolute as a request. He could see that Poppy heard it too, saw despair, frustration, dejection fleck the green of her eyes. 'After all, as you said, you can talk to Greg and anyone else here on video call. Check in every day as many times as you want.'

Hell. He couldn't risk this being the deal breaker.

'Then, as long as Greg is sure he's OK with that, I'm in.' Aware of Petra's ice-blue eyes on him, he turned to Poppy. 'Copenhagen, here we come.'

'Fabulous.' Petra beamed at them both. 'And it'll be nice for the two of you as well—give you a chance to catch up on that friendship.'

Nathan took a moment away from inner panic to eye the blonde woman with suspicion, but Petra met his gaze without guile.

'Absolutely,' he said.

'Absolutely,' echoed Poppy.

'Excellent,' Petra said briskly. 'I'll leave you to sort out details. I'm away in New York for a few days so how about we reconvene in a week? And no publicity yet—not until or unless we approve the proposal.'

'Agreed,' Poppy said and Nathan could only admire the breadth of her smile.

'Sounds good,' he lied and rose to his feet. 'I'll give you a lift home.'

Ten minutes later they were out of the gates and out of the view of the CCTV cameras. Poppy exhaled deeply and leant back on the seat.

'I don't know what to do first. Thank you or apologise or ask why. Why did you do it?'

'I… I don't know. I was trying to help, to give you a chance. I mean, I had no idea the whole thing would escalate to a trip to Copenhagen.'

Next to him he heard her sudden gurgle of laughter. 'You should have seen your face when they suggested you go too.'

'I imagine it mirrored yours.' He couldn't help it. He laughed too, the sensation a bit like pulling out an old forgotten, much-loved coat from mothballs—he and Poppy had shared so much laughter. Once. Until she'd dropped him, without warning, as if their friendship had been nothing but a figment of his imagination. Hell, maybe it had. The reminder enough to bring mirth to a close, recall that their new partnership was strictly temporary. Forged by mistake, not choice, a prelude to a permanent separation. 'But now we are committed to going, we need to figure out how it will work.'

'We do. But first, I meant it. Thank you. You did make all the difference. First by saying you'd vouch for me and then agreeing to come to Copenhagen—I could see how much it reassured Petra. Without you giving up your time, getting involved, I'd have lost this chance.'

Discomfort threatened; the knowledge he'd

stepped up for Poppy caused an edge of guilt. He could almost hear Alexis's voice. *'Told you. You were never there for me. But now it's Poppy in trouble, there you are. Giving her the time you never gave me. Even though she left you behind.'*

'It's fine. And it isn't what either of us wanted but it is as it is.' The words snapped and he sensed her flinch, forced himself to relax his voice. 'But now let me know what I've let myself in for.'

'Realistically I think I'll need four days in Copenhagen. I'll book appointments to see various venues, check out hotels and get a feel for the place. I'll work out costs and practicalities and back-up plans dependent on weather and times of year. Then I'll showcase the "best options" and summarise the rest.'

'Understood.'

'I'll need a couple of days to get everything sorted and booked.'

'OK. Let me know which hotel and I'll meet you there.' Perhaps it was foolish but travelling separately would reduce the time they spent together, a sop to offer his guilt that he was doing this at all. He pulled up outside her block of flats, turned to look at her.

Poppy gave a small tentative smile. 'So I'll see you in Copenhagen.'

'It's a date.' *No, no, no.* 'Well, not a date as in a date…it's a…'

'Time and place to meet,' she supplied and as they looked at each other he couldn't help it. The absurdity struck him and he grinned. And she smiled.

'It sounds like a joke. When is a date not a date?'

'When it's a fig.'

And then they were both laughing. And this time that coat didn't feel so full of mothballs and this time he could see her as she laughed. See the faint endearing lines round her green eyes, the dimple on her cheek and the sparkle in her eyes. *Enough.* He didn't want to start enjoying her company. This trip to Copenhagen was a mistake, something he had not wanted, something to endure, not enjoy. Anything else would be a betrayal of Alexis's memory.

'Right. I'll see you in a couple of days.'

'You will. And, Nathan? Thank you again.'

He managed a smile, waited until she got out and even raised his hand in a wave. Watched as she walked to her front door and entered and then he slammed the car into drive and took off. Work—he'd go and bury himself in work. Crack the formula, make a deal, come up with a new project, relook at the budget Envii. Whatever it took. Remind himself of his own addiction. To work, money, success. Remind himself what his life was about.

Copenhagen and Poppy would be a blip, nothing more.

Poppy looked around her hotel room, walked over to the window and looked out at the dusky city skyline, the slim tapered spires alternating with the illuminated undulating rooftops. She took a deep breath as she mentally ran through the to-do list for the next packed few days. She turned away from the view and sat at the desk in the comfort of the ergonomic chair, pulled out her phone and tried to decide whether she should tell Bella about this opportunity or not.

No. Not yet. Her friend was in rehab and she needed to focus on herself, on staying sober. This wasn't a done deal yet and it would be wrong to get Bella's hopes up at this stage.

Before she could put her phone away it buzzed. Nathan.

'Hi. I've checked in. Room 115.'

Nathan was here and the knowledge set her heart beating a little faster. She'd been almost sure he wouldn't turn up, would manufacture an excuse that would appease Petra and a strategy that allowed him to remain in London, or go anywhere else on earth except Copenhagen.

Because Poppy knew that Nathan did not

want to be here, had sensed it in the car two nights before and definitely got that vibe from their ensuing messages.

But here he was and she didn't know how she felt. Hurt that he still wanted nothing to do with her, confusion because she'd caught glimpses of their friendship re-emerging and an ever-growing perplexed panic over her hormones' ridiculous reaction to him.

This had to stop. She needed to feel precisely nothing. Nathan was from her past, he wanted nothing to do with her and that was that. Her eyes fell on the to-do list. This was the most important thing; the wedding proposal had to be her sole focus, her utmost priority. And therefore she needed Nathan because she needed his input.

She picked up her phone.

Could we meet—perhaps over dinner—to assess restaurant and to discuss itinerary for next few days?

Sure. Meet in an hour?

See you then.

For the next forty-five minutes Poppy focused on work, made sure she had a grasp on the plans for the next few days so she could explain them succinctly to Nathan and impress him with her professionalism. Professional, business. That was the theme of the evening.

And so, with her work done, she dressed accordingly. Her red hair was pulled back in a severe, smooth bun. Tailored grey suit, silk bouse tucked in at the waist offset with a statement necklace, chunky and purposeful, a glint of gold around her neck. Poppy looked at her reflection in approval.

Picking up her slimline briefcase, she slipped her feet into high-heeled black shoes with a gold buckle. Right. She was ready.

Five minutes later she entered the hotel dining room and glanced around. First impressions were favourable: the rooftop restaurant had a laid-back, boho feel to it. Overhead plants gave an impression of lushness, there was vibrant yet non-obtrusive art on the walls and the mix of booth-style seating and tables and chairs gave a sense of choice and non-uniformity. Thought had been given to the layout and the tables ensured a level of privacy whilst maximising space. A staff member appeared immediately and she was led to a table where Nathan was already sitting.

And there it was—the boom of her heart, the skip of her breath as he rose to his feet in one lithe movement. Poppy lurched to a stop—what now? She should have rehearsed this—should they shake hands, exchange air kisses? What should she do?

Nathan appeared equally frozen, his grey eyes held arrest and she could see her own helter-skelter of emotion mirrored, saw and for an instant revelled in the appreciation she saw in the grey depths.

The waiter cleared his throat and now panic entered the mix and she tore her eyes away, became aware of the light heft of her briefcase. Business. This was business. Automatically she held a hand out, her voice a croak. 'Good to see you. Thanks for meeting with me.'

He nodded. 'No problem.' He looked down at her outstretched hand and she'd swear he gulped before reaching out to take it in his. It took everything she had not to show her reaction. The feel of his cool fingers around hers shot volts of sensation through her, tingled her skin and sent a tremor of desire through her veins. And it wasn't only her; she sensed his shock, saw a tinge of colour shade his jawline, and saw the tension in his body.

Let go—her brain attempted to issue the order, but her fingers were reluctant to comply. The clatter of plates nearby brought her back to reality. Restaurant. Public. Business. Step-

ping back, she dropped his hand, and somehow
managed to move to her seat, though coordinat-
ing the act of sitting seemed ridiculously hard.

On automatic she accepted the menu from
the waiter, smiled a thank you, waited for him
to move away and forced herself to look at Nathan, saw the hooded expression in his eyes,
sensed his wariness. She tried to quell the aftermath of the disastrous handshake with objectiv-
ity. Clearly the business theme hadn't occurred
to him; he looked more…mad scientist. His
blond hair was sticking up, shower damp but
as though he'd been sitting head in hands after,
he had dark circles under his eyes and she was
aware of a strange sense of familiarity, déjà vu.
She realised she was looking at an older version of the Nathan she'd once known.

'Project breakthrough?' she enquired, the
question instinctive, and surprise crossed his
face as he nodded.

'I thought so but I was wrong. But I'm maybe
a step closer. The best thing I can do now is…'

'Distract yourself. Well, it's your lucky evening. I'm here to provide all the distraction you
need.'

Really, Poppy? She'd just thought she was
coming back from the handshake and now…
now she'd made herself sound as though she
were offering herself up as distraction and the

only type of distraction that came to her mind
was singularly inappropriate. She knew what
she'd meant, knew too that somehow instead
of businesslike the words had sounded…flirta-
tious, weighted with double entendre and hidden meaning. *Talk fast.* Before it was too late
and it got so awkward there was no salvage
possible.

'With my list. I have lists of things we need
to do. An agenda of distraction.'

He looked like a man handed a lifeline. 'Perfect. That's exactly what I need. Something else
to focus on.'

Their gazes caught and she'd swear she saw
a flash of desire, a wish he could focus on her.
Had she imagined it? She couldn't be sure. But
if she hadn't…then what?

Then nothing. This was ridiculous—this was
Nathan, a man who wasn't even interested in
being acquainted with her any more. In fact
now his expression had darkened, his lips set
in a grim line of…exasperation. Because he
was attracted to her and didn't want to be? In
which case the attraction was mutual. And despite herself that idea gave her a small thrill.
And now the silence was threatening awkward
again.

'Right. Let's focus on my lists, then.'

'Where shall we start?'

'Here at the hotel. I picked this one as it is known to be eco-friendly, which I assume is important to Greg, seeing as he works for Envii, which is all about the environment. After extensive research—I've looked up literally thousands of customer reviews—I think this fits but I'd really value your expert opinion. To assess how eco it *really* is—does it live up to the hype and the promises on the website?'

'I can do that.'

'Perfect. I've also done a general checklist—the type I do for any venue—cleanliness, customer service, ambiance, noise, views, comfort, and then of course there is the food. And more specifically I need your input on Greg and Petra. You know them. I don't. Normally I spend way more time getting to know my clients. So that's one of my biggest worries here. What if I pick somewhere and the décor is all red and Petra loathes the colour? Or somewhere like here, with this amazing rooftop bar, but she hates heights?'

She came to a stop, hoped her spiel of words had driven the forces of attraction into retreat, sure that Nathan looked a little more relaxed.

The waiter approached and she realised she hadn't even looked at the menu. Glanced down at the small à la carte section and the recommended option of a sharer menu. Gritted her teeth.

'Would you mind opting for the sharer menu? That way we can sample more of the food on offer and...'

'Realistically Greg and Petra are likely to order it so you want to check presentation, amounts, et cetera.'

'Yup.'

'That's fine by me.'

But she could see by the clench of his jaw that the same discomfort edged him. Which wasn't surprising really—the sharer menu was designed for couples, featured oysters and caviar.

Poppy scanned the cocktail menu. 'I feel in need of a cocktail.'

'Good idea.'

'OK. What do you reckon? You may like the espresso martini. It's got a secret twist.'

He raised his eyebrows as he looked down. 'Another ingredient is "bad boy" coffee liqueur.'

Their gazes met and she gave a sudden giggle. 'No way. That decides it, then, I guess. I'll watch with interest what happens after you drink it.'

'So you're assuming I'm good and the cocktail will turn me bad? I'm not sure if that's a compliment or an insult.'

'However you choose to take it.' She grinned. 'Plus, maybe I thought it was the other way round. Maybe you'll morph from villain to superhero.'

OK. What was going on here? The banter felt natural, but different from their banter of old. This held an edge, an added layer of something…elusive and unsettling. That caused her tummy to do a little dip and lurch. Added a sparkle to the air.

'I guess we'll have to wait and see,' he said. 'What are you having?'

She looked at the menu. 'The one with vodka and passionfruit.'

'The Bring on the Pass—' His voice broke off and then he resumed, and somehow now his voice seemed deeper, the words rippling over her skin. 'Bring on the Passion. Good choice.'

There it was again, the shimmer of the words between them, and it was with relief she heralded the arrival of the waiter.

They waited in silence for their cocktails, a silence edged with possibilities, not uncomfortable exactly but she felt a sense of anticipation, though she wasn't sure what she was anticipating.

She had to get a grip. Once her drink arrived

she took a sip, welcomed the bite of the vodka and the sweetness of the fruit juice. 'So,' she said. 'This is all a bit weird, right? You and me sitting here after all these years having dinner. I didn't see this coming.'

'No.' His voice was even but his agreement was a reminder that, not only had he not foreseen it, it was also his worst nightmare. He wanted her out of his life. And that idea stung, enough that Poppy was fuelled with a sudden desire to remind him that they had once had something real, worthwhile.

Enough. Nathan was helping her out here, whatever his motives. 'But, expected or not, I'd like to say thank you. I know this isn't an ideal scenario but I appreciate your help. And I apologise that it now involves sharing a menu that involves oysters.' Really? Had there been a need to mention the damn oysters?

'I don't have a problem with the oysters. Hell, I like oysters,' he said. He grinned and the effect was electric; the smile softened his face, crinkled his eyes and sent a hot rush through her body. 'I'll watch with interest what happens after you eat them.'

Hearing her own words of before quoted back at her, seeing his smile, she couldn't help it—laughter bubbled to the surface. 'Ha-ha!'

'Seriously, though, if it helps I can tell you some other facts about oysters?'

'You can? You're telling me you're an oyster expert?' She raised an eyebrow and a smile curled at the corner of her mouth.

'Yup. Actually there is so much more to oysters than most people think.'

'There is? Tell me.'

'Well, for starters, the Danes have been eating oysters since the Stone Age. Oyster shells have been found on archaeological sites dating back to 4000 BC. Can you imagine that?'

Poppy closed her eyes; she could imagine exactly that. Only she was picturing a cave, a rock table and the flicker of a fire. And a man and a woman clad in animal skins, eating oysters, before the man slung the woman caveman-style over his shoulder and… She opened her eyes hurriedly and managed, 'Any other oyster facts?'

'Plenty. There is an annual oyster festival, dedicated to the oyster—you can go on oyster safaris and eat as many oysters as you like, unpolluted, non-transported. And the more you eat the better—because the Pacific Oyster has been classed as an invasive species. They didn't originate here and they eat the food supply that nature actually provided for other species, including migratory birds. So if they are allowed to multiply it has a knock-on effect. So eating them actually keeps nature balanced.'

The enthusiasm in his voice was infectious and she realised she seemed way too focused on the mouth uttering the words, the way his fingers curled round his glass.

'I'd forgotten this about you.'

'What?'

'The way you are a walking encyclopaedia.' His brain was interested in so many different topics and ideas, buzzing with curiosity and scraps of information that he would call on to help him figure out some scientific or engineering conundrum. Or in this case to bail them out of an awkward situation.

He shook his head. 'Sorry. I didn't mean to bore you.'

'You're not. At all.' In her eagerness to reassure him she reached out without thinking, put her hand over his, and she couldn't help the small gasp at the shock of contact, the fizz, bang, electric pop. And he felt it too; she saw the reaction, the sense of shock mirrored in his expression, as they both looked down at their hands. 'At all. At all,' she repeated, pulling her hand away as the waiter arrived.

'Here you are,' he said. 'Made to our chef's signature recipe, seasoned with chilli and lime so they have both heat and zing that complement the taste perfectly. Enjoy.'

Heat and zing. Just what they needed. 'Right. Time for the taste test.' Her voice was resonant with a false heartiness. She picked up the tiny fork and made sure the oyster was detached. 'The next question though. To chew or swallow?' Talk about loaded—the question sounded ridiculously suggestive.

'Chew,' he said, and she could hear a rasp in his voice as if he was striving to sound normal. 'Another oyster fact. That releases the briny taste. But apparently you should only chew once or twice. So here goes.'

He picked up the oyster shell in a salute, and she followed suit, mesmerised now as she watched him eat it, watched the strong column of his throat as he swallowed, and as she did the same and the heat and tang of lime and the cold salt of the oyster combined she couldn't help the shiver that ran over her skin.

They couldn't help the level of awareness, every heightened sense, as they continued to eat the succession of dishes, they sampled the exquisite luxury of the caviar served on tiny blinis, its fresh ocean taste cutting through the unexpected buttery richness of the blini, followed by the vegan satay, in which the silky texture of the tofu perfectly balanced the crunch of the peanut sauce.

Afterwards she couldn't even remember what they spoke about. Spice and portion size, the fact that this caviar was sourced from a farm renowned for its adherence to environmental rules, but even as their lips formed syllables and strung them into sentences something else was happening. She could see it in the way his intent grey eyes watched her, the way her own gaze focused on detail, the sculpt of his forearm, the way one errant blond curl of hair rested on his jawline, the way his grey eyes lingered a fraction too long on her lips.

And then the final choice—the dessert. 'This is delicious.' The words were stilted now, as the flow of desperate talk could no longer be sustained. 'Better than delicious,' she continued. 'Light, creamy and visually incredible.' The matcha tea panna cotta a delicate green.

'Definitely delicious,' Nathan agreed. The words were deep and somehow conveyed the idea that he wasn't talking about the damn dessert. 'And not too heavy.'

'Agreed.' Her mouth was on automatic now. 'I still feel alert and ready for action—' She broke off, a flush climbing her cheekbones.

'Which is handy on a honeymoon,' he deadpanned. He shrugged. 'It's true, isn't it? We're trying to assess whether this is a good place to spend your wedding night and honeymoon. So we have to think about the...' another shrug and she watched the lift of muscles as one mesmerised '...practicalities.'

Poppy gulped; the game—if that was what it was, and the idea gave her a funny little thrill—had upped a level. Though she sensed it had just happened, that this was spinning out of their control, and she didn't care. 'We do. You'll be glad to know I've asked the manager if we can see the honeymoon suite, for that very reason. To assess its *practicalities*. After all, you wouldn't want a squeaky bed.'

'Or a lumpy mattress.'

'Exactly. That's why we're going to check it out.' *Oh, hell*. That sounded ridiculously suggestive.

The waiter arrived to clear the plates. 'Coffee?' he asked. 'Another drink?'

Temptation beckoned, the idea of sitting here with Nathan, continuing the shimmer of flirtatious chat, nigh on irresistible. *Oh, God*. What was she thinking? What was she doing? What had happened to *business*?

'I'm good, thanks,' she said, and turned to Nathan once the waiter had left. 'I'm going for a walk. I'd like to get a feel of Copenhagen by night.' She felt the urge to clear her head. 'I'm pretty sure Petra and Greg will want to do a romantic moonlit stroll so that's my plan. But, honestly, you don't need to do this bit. I know you have work to do. We can meet in the morning.'

CHAPTER FIVE

NATHAN KNEW WHAT he should do. In the interests of self-preservation he should let Poppy go on her own. It was late but not that late and Poppy was a grown woman completely capable of looking out for herself; moreover she wasn't a fool, she would be walking in still populated, busy streets. So there was no need to play the protective male and yet he felt protective. An inner voice pointed out it was a lot more than that—even if Poppy had her own personal bodyguard Nathan would still want to go with her. But Poppy didn't have a bodyguard and, old-fashioned or not, Nathan was going to indulge his protective instinct.

After all… 'Actually I've heard Nyhavn by night is a must-see, so if you don't mind I'll tag along.'

There was a heartbeat of hesitation and then she nodded. 'Sure. I'll just go and change into something warmer.'

'Fine. I'll meet you in the lobby.'

Fifteen minutes later she approached him, the business dress replaced by jeans and a light bright red coat cinched with a belt. And he couldn't help the look of appreciation in his eyes, couldn't even hide it—she was so damned beautiful.

Half an hour later and they'd reached the cobbled streets of the harbour, flanked with beautifully lit, brightly coloured houses. The vibrant yellow, blue, red and terracotta walls dazzled the eye. 'Wow,' Poppy breathed. 'Just wow. It's so vibrant and alive.'

As she was, and that was how she made him feel. And that was the problem—over dinner he'd felt different, as though it were OK to banter and laugh and enjoy. But it wasn't. He knew that too.

'And yet also so full of history.' Think facts, dry, cold facts. 'Those town houses are built with wood, bricks, and plaster. The oldest house, number nine, dates from 1681.'

She nodded. 'The harbour was started work on in 1670 and it took five years and it was actually dug by prisoners of war, Swedish, I think. And later on Hans Christian Andersen lived here for years.'

As they walked, side by side through necessity given the number of people, he was so aware of her proximity. The scent of her shampoo, her warmth. Aware too of the immense care they were both taking not to so much as brush hands. What were they scared of? Combustion, for Pete's sake?

She turned. 'And look over there,' she said, pointing to the other side of the canal, 'That's known as the shady side and that's where all the mansions are.'

'Including the Charlottenborg Palace. Though it isn't exactly a fairy-tale palace.'

'No.' She stopped to study it. 'But it's pretty big. And probably easier to run and maintain. So whoever designed it probably knew better than to believe in fairy tales.'

He turned away now and looked down at her, caught the note of bitterness, knew she had too as she gave a small laugh. 'Listen to me. Clearly I belong to the bah humbug variety of wedding planner.'

'So you don't believe in fairy tales?' he asked.

'No. I don't. But that doesn't mean I don't believe in happy marriages. But fairy tales aren't…real. And most people don't live in palaces. And even if they do it doesn't mean they are happy. Lots of real marriages take place in small, cramped one-bedroom apartments, or modest terraced houses where the bills have to be paid and two people go out to work to put food on the table and that's reality. And it's a damn sight more important to be able to deal with reality than it is to have some rose-coloured dream of life in a palace. Because the trappings don't make a real prince.'

As she spoke her pace quickened and she suddenly stumbled as a glass dropped from one of the tables rolled off and under her feet.

Instantly he reached out, grasped her arm to steady her, an arm where she'd pushed up the sleeves of the coat so his fingers encircled her bare skin as he pulled her back and into his body.

Oh, hell. Combustion was nothing on it. She was so close, her body against his, her red hair tickling his nose, his hand still on her arm, and it felt as though she were scorching him, an inverse branding, and as she turned, still so close somehow, he was still encircling her with an arm looped round her waist, and now she looked up at him, her green eyes wide and questioning, and all he wanted to do was kiss her. Nothing else mattered.

'Excuse me.' The voice pulled him back to reality. What was he doing? What was he thinking?

The man standing in front of them looked ever so slightly the worse for drink, signs Nathan recognised all too well from his mother. 'Excuse me,' he said again, with an endearing smile. 'I wanted to check you were all right. That was my bottle, you see, and I dropped it. Luckily it was empty,' he added.

'I'm completely fine. Thank you,' Poppy said. 'Don't give it another thought.'

'Thank you.' The man swayed slightly. 'Have a lovely evening. In this wonderful city.' He leant forward confidingly. 'And, so you know, that café there does wonderful coffee. When I've had one more beer that's where I'm headed.' With that he gave a wave and headed towards the nearest bar.

They waited and Nathan wondered if they could possibly pretend the moment hadn't happened. He knew they couldn't, but before he could say anything Poppy nodded towards the café. 'Let's take his advice. Grab a coffee. It's a bit late for caffeine but, hey-ho, let's live dangerously.'

'I think we're already doing that,' Nathan said under his breath as they headed into the small buzzing café. Surrounded by the sound of conversation and laughter, the clink of glass and the chink of cutlery on plates, he slowed down. 'We need to talk.'

Five minutes later, coffee cups in hand, they sat at the water's edge overlooking the canal. They both studied the wooden ships that lined the harbour, as if to marshal their forces for the conversation ahead.

'That wasn't very clever of us,' she said at last.

'No, it wasn't.' He could hear the harshness of his tone, the coldness.

'I don't understand it.' The frustration was evident in her voice as she turned to him. 'How can you and I be attracted to each other?' Her eyes widened suddenly. 'That is what is happening, isn't it? What we need to talk about. Please, please, please, feel free to tell me I've got it wrong.'

How he wanted to tell her she had but honesty compelled the words. 'You're not wrong.' The words were wrenched from him. 'Though God knows I wish you were.' He had no idea how to deal with this, the guilt of it, the fact he couldn't simply stamp it out, control it. 'I don't want to feel this way, believe me.'

'Trust me, neither do I. I need to be focused on this wedding proposal. Not some ludicrous, ridiculous attraction that doesn't even make sense. In all our years of friendship there was never anything like this. We were friends, nothing more at all.'

'Perhaps the key to that sentence is tense. We were friends. We haven't been friends for years. Not since you walked away.' He could still remember the hurt he'd felt, the deep, searing sense of loss.

He heard her catch her breath as she turned to him. 'That's not fair. I didn't walk away. You told me to go, you wouldn't even let me over your threshold. And I got that. You'd just lost Alexis, lost your wife, and you were distraught.' She raised a hand to prevent him from speaking. 'And maybe now is the one chance I'll get to say this. I am so sorry, so very, very sorry, for your loss. Losing Alexis, the love of your life, must have been devastating. I understand I turned up too soon. But after that, in the months and years since… I didn't understand at first why you wouldn't let me in. But then I figured it out—you don't want any reminders of the past at all because it's too painful.'

Her voice was low, brimmed with compassion and sympathy, and in one sense she was right. The past was a minefield for him, tripped with guilt and regret, for all the ways he'd failed Alexis. He'd got marriage all wrong, judged it by the wrong measures and bars and Alexis had paid the price.

'Which is fair enough. But what isn't fair is to say that I walked away from our friendship.'

'But you did,' he said simply. 'You walked away long before Alexis died. You walked away before my marriage. You didn't even come to the wedding.'

There was a dead silence and he knew, knew then that something was wrong. Poppy had gone very still next to him; he could almost hear the whir and strum of her brain working, sifting.

'Poppy. Look at me. Please,' he added, and he saw reluctance in the slowness of her movement. He studied her closely, aware even now of her beauty, her red hair dappled in the street lights, the serious expression in her green eyes as they met his, guarded and wary and a little bit shocked. 'What did I say?'

'Nothing.' He watched her closely, saw her hand reach up to curl a tendril of hair round her finger, saw the telltale crease on one side of her mouth.

'You never were a good liar.'

'I'm not lying.'

'Yes, you are. I did say something. Something that surprised you, shocked you, and you're trying to figure out what to do about it.'

She sighed then, turned away to look out at the water. 'It doesn't matter. What's done is done, the past is over and done with. It's the future that matters.'

'Agreed. But... I have always wondered why you walked away from our friendship.' Wondered long and hard, the hurt real. But he'd accepted it, believed he'd got it wrong with Poppy, misjudged the strength of their friendship. As he'd got it wrong with his father. He'd believed his dad loved him; he'd been wrong. He'd believed Poppy was a true friend; he'd been wrong. Proof in the fact they'd both elected to walk away, to stop seeing him.

But now…perhaps he'd been wrong about Poppy and, damn it… 'It does matter to me. So I am asking now for the truth. Why did you abandon our friendship?'

'I didn't.' She looked at him, her eyes wide in the moonlight. The sounds of the bar-goers and the strolling tourists seemed to fade as she spoke. 'Is that what you thought? That I just upped and left?' There was disbelief in her voice.

'That's what you told me,' he pointed out. 'We met for a drink and you told me you were on your way to the airport, taking off, going travelling. To work out what to do with your life.'

'I *was* trying to work out what I wanted to do with my life.'

'But you didn't discuss it with me, your best friend.'

'It wasn't *appropriate* to discuss it with you.' The words were pulled from her and these ones he believed.

'Why not?'

She let out a sigh, sipped her coffee and looked at it as if she wished it were something stronger.

'Because part of the reason I was going was you. I thought it was what you wanted.'

'That makes no sense—why would you think that?'

'You'd just met Alexis and I didn't want to get in the way.'

'You thought I couldn't have a friend *and* a girlfriend? That I wanted you to cut me out of your life?'

'I thought you wanted me to back off. I thought that's what you wanted because that's what Alexis told me.'

'Alexis?'

She exhaled a breath. 'You really didn't know?' Again there was disbelief.

'Why would I lie? I have no idea what you are talking about.' Though he was beginning to think he could make a pretty good guess.

'Alexis told me that you didn't want to hurt my feelings but you needed space, that the intensity of our friendship was affecting your relationship with Alexis, that you wanted to spend more time with her exclusively and our friendship was getting in the way. That she knew I understood that relationships meant that friendships changed, became less important, but you were worried I wouldn't get it and would be upset. So she was talking to me instead, because you couldn't face hurting my feelings.'

Nathan stared at her as emotions fast-tracked. The first one of anger that Alexis had done that, spoken in his name, given him words he'd never spoken, never even thought of. Followed by sheer disbelief at his own obtuseness—he'd had no idea that Alexis had felt threatened, no idea she'd actually spoken to Poppy, no idea that this was behind Poppy's defection. Obtuse didn't cover it. And alongside anger was sadness for Alexis, that her fear of Poppy had been seeded so early. Anger with himself for accepting Poppy's disappearance so tamely. But also anger with Poppy.

'I didn't know. You should have said something. You trusted the words of a woman you barely knew, who I barely knew at that point, over a friendship of years. You walked away from our friendship, gave up, judged me to be too inept to be your friend. Without even consulting me.'

'Yes. Yes, I did. I did believe Alexis.' The words so loaded with emotion he flinched. 'And, yes, I thought she was speaking for you, but I understand why she did what she did and

I think she was right. And I still think I was right to go.'

'Couldn't you have backed off slightly, seen me less often? Instead of leaving completely—surely Alexis didn't ask you to do that.'

'No, she didn't.'

'Then I was still right. You walked away. If you'd cared you wouldn't have done that.'

'I did it because I cared,' she shot back and now there was anger in her voice. Anger and sincerity. But her green eyes were shadowed now too. 'And in the end the important thing is that you and Alexis were happy, and that is worth *everything*. That you had that time together.'

Pain touched him—Alexis hadn't been happy. And right now neither was Poppy. Because he could see pain in her green eyes, ghosts and demons that he had awoken with his questions, and now he couldn't leave her to face them alone. Wanted to help put them back to rest, back in the past where Poppy had wanted to keep them.

'That is important, but I still don't understand. Why did you walk away? Why did it have to be all or nothing? I should have asked then. I didn't. But I am asking now. Tell me.'

CHAPTER SIX

POPPY LOOKED AT HIM, saw that he meant it, his grey eyes serious, completely focused on her. He wanted to know why she had walked away, why she had taken Alexis's words so much to heart that she had removed herself completely from his life. The idea that he hadn't wanted her to go, hadn't even wanted her to back off, changed so much about her memories of their friendship. Part of her wished she'd known back then, even though she knew in the end it would have made no difference. She still would have gone.

But did she want to tell him why? It wasn't the sort of thing they had ever spoken about before. Back then their talk had always been about the future, their hopes and dreams and determination to succeed. Or more prosaically about which film to see, where to go and hang out, with the tacit understanding that neither wanted to return home.

But now, sitting here under the stars, the lap of water from the canal, the brightly coloured buildings at their back, she knew that she had to tell him. Her actions had hurt him; for years he'd believed she'd abandoned him and he deserved to know why.

'I left because I believed it was the right thing to do. I knew it was from experience. You see, that was the secret to my mum's successful second marriage.'

'I don't understand.'

'You knew my mum and I weren't close. We never have been because she believes her marriage to my father failed because of me, that my father first strayed because she was pregnant. Continued to stray because he didn't want to face the responsibility of parenthood.'

'But she can't blame you for your father's actions. That's…plain wrong.'

Poppy shrugged. 'It's also true. My dad is a serial womaniser, he would have strayed at some point, but it is highly likely the pregnancy was a catalyst. My dad is also an egotist, and he would have felt displaced by my arrival. That in turn made him ripe for the plucking. The woman who persuaded him to divorce my mother and marry her did it when I was less than a year old. My mum was humiliated and furious and heartbroken and she believed that if she hadn't had me it would all have been different. And so she stopped loving me. Or at least that's what I think happened—maybe she never loved me in the first place. I don't remember her hugging me, not once.'

Her voice cracked, but she held a hand out to stop him responding, knew if he uttered sympathy she'd cry. 'Anyway. When I was three she met my stepfather, Donald, and she was absolutely determined that history would not repeat. So she pretty much "disappeared me"— shunted me back to my father and when that wasn't possible, because Dad didn't want me either, she moved me round friends and family. Kept me completely in the background. Even after they got married, I was very much a visitor, and when I was seven I went to boarding school. Which was probably the best thing for me. But my point is that it *worked*. My mum's second marriage is really happy—she and Don have got three kids and they are a happy family. But there isn't space for me in that bubble. There never was.'

'And so you thought there wasn't space for you in my relationship?'

'Exactly. As soon as Alexis spoke to me I could see it. I couldn't be the third wheel that clogged up the works, the person who got in the way. I couldn't be the catalyst to ruin another marriage. So a clean break seemed the best way. But I never meant to hurt you. I thought you knew Alexis had spoken to me and when you didn't question my going I thought you were pleased.'

'I wasn't and I wish, I really wish I had questioned you. But you need to know that your mum was wrong,' he said fiercely. 'Wrong to make you feel like that. Wrong to not put you first, wrong to lay blame on you for your father's shortcomings and her own. Your father did not have to cheat, he chose to. Your mother could have chosen to include you in a new relationship, should have seen that any man who is willing to sideline a child isn't worth a look.'

'She may be wrong but she's happy. You can't argue with that or the fact that if she could turn back time she wouldn't choose to have me. It's that simple. I haven't made her life better in any way. In truth she doesn't owe me anything—you don't have to like someone just because you're related to them. But I am here, I do exist, and I won't apologise for that. That's why I look forward.'

'And I admire that. But you are not at fault.' His voice was urgent.

'Nathan, it's OK. I've come to terms with it. I know it's not my fault. And truly, the most important thing is that you and Alexis were happy and if my going helped that, then that is a good thing. Right?'

She'd swear he hesitated as he turned to look out over the canal. Then he nodded. 'Yes, that's a good thing, but… I don't want you to believe that your absence resulted in our happiness.'

'Even if maybe it did? If Alexis benefited then I'm good with that. I couldn't have coped with being a spanner in the works.'

A shadow crossed his eyes. He opened his mouth and closed it again.

'I was the unwitting cause of my mother's unhappiness. I didn't want history to repeat.'

'There was no need for your mother to be unhappy. You could have brought her great happiness. Your mother missed out. Big time. And she still is now.'

That aspect had never occurred to her. 'You think?'

'I know so. She missed out on knowing you, spending time with you, and she lost out. I know that.'

The sweetness of the words, his palpable desire to make her feel better, warmed her and without thinking she leaned over and brushed her lips against his cheek. 'Thank you.'

He lifted his hand, cupped her cheek and they both froze. The gentle touch, the exquisite sweetness of sensation seemed to still time, create an instant that felt timeless, a moment to treasure. And now she wanted to kiss him again, only this time she wanted to brush her lips against his.

Oh, God. She pulled backwards, stared at him wide-eyed. 'We seem to have come full circle.'

'Yes.' The admission was low, vibrant now not with anger but with confusion and sadness. Then he ran a hand through his hair and took a deep breath. 'So we need to figure out what to do about it. We're two intelligent people—we can get past this for the next few days.'

'Words,' Poppy said. 'The question is how?' She thought, figured she knew the answer. The same as it always was. 'I think the best way is avoidance. If we don't see each other, then we don't spark the attraction.' Yet somehow the thought of not seeing Nathan over the next days, of brief sterile meetings, seemed...flat. But it was the right thing to do. Absence solved problems.

He considered her words and she sensed he could see the logic, the wisdom of them and then he shook his head. 'No. There must be another way. I am not buying into your mum's theory, not letting you "disappear" yourself to make things better. Plus I want to help with this proposal and I want to honour my promise to

Petra and Greg. So we will figure out a different solution.'

Warmth touched her at his words, the idea that he would choose this option over the easy one, the logical one. Stop or she'd be tempted to lean over and kiss him again. Instead she tried to keep her tone light. 'Such as?'

'We ignore it.'

She stared at him. 'That's your big plan. We ignore it.'

'Yes. We've acknowledged it exists, we have no intention of acting on it, so we ignore it. It's only for a few days, after all.'

A wholly irrational hurt hovered that he still wanted to end their friendship even as she realised this new attraction made it even more sensible that they did so. Even as a little voice suddenly questioned why this attraction was such a bad thing. Ridiculous question. It was a bad thing because Nathan was still in love with Alexis. That was the bottom line. Poppy was a reminder of his past, a link to Alexis, and he wanted her gone.

So, 'You're right. We ignore it. And if we do it will just fade away.' Poppy pushed down the big question—*how* were they supposed to ignore it?—as redundant. The clue was in the meaning of the word. If you ignored something you pretended it wasn't happening, looked away, didn't react. Easy.

'Good. We are two adults and we are in Copenhagen to do a job. Together. So let's do it.' He rose to his feet and reached out a hand to help her get up.

Poppy tried to hide her hesitation. A part of her wanted to put her hand in his, the other part wondered if it were wise. It would be fine, because even if there was a reaction, a spark, it didn't matter because they could ignore it.

That was the master plan, the only plan.

So she braced for impact and put her hand in his, and pretended with all her might that she felt nothing, that the cool clasp, the strength of his fingers, the glimpse of his wrist as she stood had no effect on her. *Ignore, ignore, ignore.* The new mantra.

CHAPTER SEVEN

Poppy opened her eyes and blinked. She felt well
rested for the first time in weeks, a vague memory of dreams, the touch of Nathan's hand, the
feel of his cheek against her lips, the closeness…
the…stop. She sat up, tried to shake off the vestiges of sleep and the linger of dreams. Presum-
ably she was supposed to ignore her dreams as
well.

Probably best, because her focus needed to be
on the day ahead, the list of tasks she'd planned.
A quick shower and she pulled on a flared
autumnal-coloured trouser suit and headed
downstairs to the dining room.

She felt a moment of embarrassment as she
approached the breakfast table. After all, last
night she had told Nathan things she'd never
told anyone.

'Hey.'

'Hey.' To her relief he sounded completely
normal and if she felt a jolt as she studied him,

blond hair shower damp, dressed in jeans and a T-shirt and looking gorgeous, she made sure not to show it. Ignore, ignore, ignore.

She gestured to the laden buffet table. 'Looks good. Let's load up.'

Minutes later they eyed each other over heaped plates. 'All organic and sustainable,' she said. 'And plentiful.' She looked down at her plate, eyed the bacon, scrambled eggs, ham, salami, cheese. 'As for the bread, it's freshly baked and looks beyond amazing.'

'I had a chat to the chef. She says her home-made yoghurt featuring acacia honey and almonds is mandatory eating, so leave room.'

Poppy looked at the menu. 'It says here a vegan menu is available on request as well.'

'I spoke to Mariella about that too and ordered it for tomorrow.'

'Count me in too. Maybe I can help. I am guessing this is all about research for your new venture. I can tell you what I think—be part of your consumer research.'

'I'll order a vegan breakfast for two, then. Thank you.'

'So tell me about it. Why a vegan project? I mean, it's completely different from electric cars. Certainly less…luxury item. Less cool.'

'I know. I've accepted being the face of the next vegan steak is not going to win me the same type of kudos. But…well, I've got Greg to be cool and he does it way better than me. At heart I am still the nerdy geek you once knew.'

She looked at him and gulped slightly. 'I don't think anyone would term you as a nerdy geek. Too much muscle for that.' Had she really said that? 'Objectively speaking. *Anyway*, that doesn't answer the question.'

'It happened by accident really. I was at a charity fundraiser to raise awareness of the environment and there was an amazing speaker there who was saying how veganism can help the planet. It caught my attention and I did some research and…'

'Off you went. It's like the time you got sidetracked into cookery. You decided to make a fry-up for breakfast and became obsessed with how to make the perfect one, then you graduated onto the "perfect pancake batter" and then to the best way to make a white sauce. And that all started because of some university challenge. I'm surprised you didn't become a chef.' She grinned at him. 'Maybe this is a direct result of that dabble in the culinary world. Only now you've bought a vegan company.'

'Yup and I am really excited about it. Environmentally there is a school of thought that says veganism is good for the planet. Business-wise it is a massively growing market. So it's win-win. And it's a challenge. I want to find the perfect alternative to steak—a vegan steak that mirrors the real thing.'

His sheer enthusiasm, the verve, the light in his eye were mesmerising. 'But surely designing a steak is a completely different branch of science from designing a car. Chemistry rather than engineering and physics.'

'It is different but I want to give it a try. That and a vegan foie gras. So that's where my brain is a lot of the time. Thinking about texture, taste, the sensory equivalent—' He broke off and his lips turned up in a small smile of rue. 'Sorry. I've gone off on one. Greg is interested in this but his heart is with cars, not plant-based food, and because it's at the early stages I haven't really been talking much about it.'

'Don't apologise. What's the point of a new project if you're not excited about it? But I'd also like to know how you did it. Set up Envii, became a billionaire CEO. When I left to go travelling you were about to do a master's degree. Before setting up your own business.'

'I abandoned that plan. Once Alexis and I got engaged we decided it made more sense for me to get a proper job, a salaried job. Start out in banking. The money was really good so that's what I decided to do.' That sounded really unlike the Nathan she'd known—that Nathan had wanted to be in control of his wealth, not reliant on a massive institution who could sack him without warning.

'I landed a great banking position and the job was going well. And then...' He shrugged. 'I got an idea. A real idea and I couldn't think of anything else. So I made a deal with Alexis. I'd stay at the bank until we'd saved a certain amount and then I'd take a sabbatical—for six months. In the meantime I took a welding course and got an additional job as a welder. Part time. I was lucky. I managed to persuade someone to take me on evenings and weekends restoring cars, though we did other work as well. It was extra money and I loved it, actually getting my hands dirty.'

Of course he had; she could picture him, oil-smudged overalls, blond hair spiked, and his focus as he learnt, stored away information, and all the while his mind would have been shaping ideas. The image sent a sudden shiver of desire through her. Desire and a fierce regret that she hadn't been there, alongside a shameful green flash of jealousy that Alexis had. *Enough.* She'd made her choice and she still believed it to have been right.

'That sounds incredible. I'd love to have a go at welding.' And she would have. 'I'd definitely have got myself a pair of overalls and joined you.' She wondered if Alexis had done exactly that.

She saw an arrest in his grey eyes, an emotion she couldn't identify; it was gone before she could even try. Surprise, regret, she didn't know. 'Anyway, go on.'

'Well, I eventually hit the savings target and I quit the banking job.'

'Abandoned the designer suit and dived back into your overalls?' The image fast-tracked in her mind and there was that shiver again.

'That sums it up. I was all ready to go. I knew I had six months to get the project off the ground, and I had all my ducks in a row. I'd secured a workshop and a business loan for machinery and so on. And I'd patented my idea—an exhaust for motorbikes and race cars that increased efficiency and reduced emissions. I knew it was a winner and it was. Production took off. It's also when I became interested, really interested, in the environment. And so Envii was born. I went from exhausts to the idea of a luxury electric car via the idea of solar panels. And here I am.'

'That sounds like an amazing, exhilarating journey. Alexis must have been proud of you. I am so glad she got to see your success, to be part of it, part of that exhilaration.'

'Yes.' The word was wooden and she knew

she must have overstepped, that the past, his past with Alexis, was a no-go area.

So, time to move the conversation on. 'I think it is amazing that you have a company that has an environmental ethos. I do always try to balance wedding plans with an eco sense. There are so many things you can do—you can buy second hand, which sounds tacky, but it isn't. You can take something vintage, or preloved, and make it uniquely yours. Or use your mum's dress, or grandmother's, design your own dress from scratch—using sustainable, local fabrics.' She paused. 'Now I'm going off on one.'

'Feel free. I'm interested in this.' He hesitated. 'I'm also interested in why you've given up on the idea of fashion. Because it seems to me that your heart, your passion, is still fashion. That that is the bit about wedding planning you love most. The dress, shoes, fabrics, what it looks like, the visual effects...'

'It's part of wedding planning, but I love my job with Star Weddings.'

'I get that, but wedding planning was Bella's dream, not yours. And it's hard for me to believe you've simply given up your dream of a career in fashion.'

His voice held genuine curiosity and she couldn't blame him. Years ago she'd loved fashion, but then she'd believed it was part of her future, a safe dream. Her mother had pulled that rug from beneath her feet. She hadn't told anybody that, not even Bella. Almost as if saying it out loud made it real, made her have to admit exactly how much her mother wished she could 'disappear' her daughter.

'I'm still interested in fashion, but as part of my job brief.' She glared at him, almost challenging him to dispute the fact.

But he didn't and perhaps that was what made her keep talking, because she could see scepticism in his grey eyes. 'And working at Star Weddings—it's mine. Nothing to do with my family name, or history. Something I can excel at in my own right. Not handed to me on a platter. I mean, look at you. You built up Envii yourself. From nothing. Built on grit and determination and talent. But it's your talent; your choices.'

He poured them both more coffee from the cafetiere as he thought. 'Sure, but you can take something already made and improve on it. Isn't that what you're talking about with redesigning wedding dresses? There's nothing wrong with inheriting a dream and expanding it.'

With difficulty she kept her body relaxed, didn't flinch at the word 'inherited', told herself it didn't matter. 'Maybe. But there's more satisfaction in achieving it from scratch. Like you did.'

'As long as it's your dream,' he said.

'It is.' It had to be. Time to close this conversation down; his grey eyes held far more scrutiny than she was comfortable with. 'And right now if I want that dream to survive I need to get on with this proposal.' She glanced at her watch. 'So this is the plan for the day. I've got appointments booked this morning with hairdressers and a make up artist. Then I've arranged for us to check out the honeymoon suite.' She frowned. 'I also want to ask your advice, but let's grab those yoghurts you mentioned first.'

Minutes later she made a small sound of appreciation. 'OK. These are incredible. The perfect amount of sweet and a crunchy, nutty seed taste complements them perfectly.'

'Organic ingredients as well,' Nathan said. 'I double-checked.'

'Thank you. I knew you'd be an asset.'

'So what other advice can I give?'

'I've been considering having the wedding ceremony in a scenic garden but I am worried that is a bit tame for Greg. I mean, he's an ex-racing driver—a man who lived life in the fast lane, a man who thrived on adrenalin and being the best at what he did. Maybe he'd like there to be more of a thrill to the day, some action in the fairy tale. I don't want the wedding to only be about Petra—it should be about both of them. I want Greg to feel we've done something for him, thought of him in some way. Maybe I could incorporate driving in some way or something really adrenalin-inducing or—'

'No.' His voice was sharp.

'Why not?' Her look was one of puzzlement.

'Because I don't think you can match the thrill of racing a car; that part of his life is over. By necessity after his accident and…' He hesitated.

She got it. 'And trying to replace it is almost condescending or will make him sad?'

'Yes.'

'OK. I get that but I'd like to think of something. Maybe I could try to do something dazzling that reminds him of his previous life—set up a casino or—'

'No!' This time his voice was too loud and she knew there was something there he wasn't telling. But that was exactly why she needed him, to stop her making any stupid, though well-meaning, decisions. 'I don't think he'd want any reminders of his old life. He's a different person now. That's how he coped with it; he's moved on and wants to keep the past in the past. So better to do something for the man he is now, the person he's become. Greg loves his life now and I'm not sure it's a good idea to try and recreate something he's had to come to terms with losing.'

She wondered if he realised the impact of his words. 'No wonder you're friends and you clearly understand exactly how he feels. I guess you can empathise because in a way that must be how you feel as well.'

'Sorry?'

'Keep the past in the past,' she said, hooking her fingers in the air to indicate quote marks. 'That's how you feel about me. You don't want any reminders either. Even now, when we've reconnected, when we've cleared up past misunderstandings, you don't want to renew our friendship, do you? Just like Greg wouldn't want to drive a race car.'

'You can't go back,' he said. 'The people we were then, they're gone. Our friendship was between the people we were then. Young, misfits, two people who needed each other then. We've changed since then, we've both been through so many of life's events both tragic and good and we're two different people now. Our friendship didn't grow and evolve with those changes and differences and that means it is a past friendship. Because that is where it belongs.'

'In the past where Alexis is too and all those

memories of pain and grief. Do you think you can do what Greg has done? Come to terms with your loss, create a new life, a new relationship?'

'I will always carry the loss with me, but I have got on with my life, like Greg has. And my life now is work. I won't revisit the idea of marriage. Or get involved in a serious relationship.'

She could see the look of near panic on his face and for some reason it made her feel… Sad. Which made no sense. It meant nothing to Poppy if Nathan Larrimore was up for a relationship of any sort. He'd made it clear he didn't want her friendship any more. If it hadn't been plain before, it was even more so now and she needed to close this conversation down, accept his decision and move on as he wished to. She shouldn't have reminded him of his grief and loss.

'Well, speaking of work, I'd better get going. There really is no need for you to come and discuss hair and make up so why don't you stay here and work, mix up compounds in the hotel room, or there is a gym here, maybe a workout will get your synapses firing? Then we can meet up back here later. Does that sound like a plan?'

'Yes, it does. Message me details of where to

meet. Oh, and I forgot to say earlier, I arranged to hire bikes today. Just ask at Reception. I thought it may be a good way to get about. Copenhagen is known for the excellence of its biking system.'

'Actually, no can do. I can't ride a bike. Never learnt.' She kept her voice casual even though it still hurt—that neither of her parents, none of her step-parents and definitely none of the nannies had ever shown any interest in teaching her how to ride a bike. She glanced at her watch. 'Anyway, I need to run. Enjoy your morning. I'll see you later.'

CHAPTER EIGHT

NATHAN GLANCED AT his watch and knocked on Poppy's door for the second time. It was definitely the time they'd arranged—he definitely hadn't got so involved in research that he'd got it wrong.

Finally he heard her call, 'Come in,' and he pushed the door open.

'Hi. Here I am, reporting for duty.'

'Great.' She sounded preoccupied as she looked up from the table where she was sitting and he studied the scene, saw that the laptop was shut and peeking out from under it was a glint of white—a piece of paper, or a notebook. Poppy followed his gaze and he'd swear a grimace of annoyance crossed her face.

'What were you doing?' he asked.

'Going through the proposal so far.' Her voice was even but there was a small telltale tic at the corner of her mouth, the Poppy Winchester 'tell', and as if she knew it she raised a hand and brushed the spot.

'Do you want me to take a look?'

'No. But thank you. I'd rather wait until I've gone through it properly.'

'Hmm.' He allowed his gaze to linger on the closed laptop, looked back up at her but she met his gaze full on. 'In full Sherlock Holmes style, I deduce that you were busy on something other than the proposal, lost track of time and when I knocked on the door you tried to hide the incriminating evidence.'

'Don't be ridiculous. There is nothing incriminating about it.' But she didn't deny it either and curiosity tugged at him. In the olden days he would have pushed harder, even gone and taken a look. In the olden days though she would have simply shown him. But this was these days, days where everything was confusing and complicated. Days where attraction shimmered and appeared with no warning. 'Right. Let's go,' she said and rose to her feet.

Five minutes later they were standing outside the door to the honeymoon suite. 'The manager gave me the key card. We've got as long as we like. But first we need to think about the approach.'

He frowned. 'I don't get it. They get out of the lift and they walk to the door, swipe the wooden key card and go in.'

She rolled her eyes. 'It's not that simple.

Every moment of this day needs to be special, needs to work for them. We need to picture exactly how it will work, the practicalities of it all. So the wedding ceremony is over, be it in a planetarium or a beautiful garden, the reception for the guests is done, let's say there's been dancing, and now they are back at the hotel. So by now I am guessing Greg's leg may be playing up a bit. So what happens if the lift is out of order? Will he be able to make it up two flights of stairs without discomfort? Because I'm guessing it will matter to Greg if he's showing what he would term as "weakness".'

Now he got it and he felt an admiration for how thorough she was being but also how much she cared. He walked over to the stairs and considered. 'He'd be OK, as long as what you have in mind for the dancing isn't strenuous.'

'Nope. I'm thinking about a jazz club where you mostly listen and probably won't dance at all. But I need to think worst-case scenario. This is the best suite but there are other suites and other hotels.' She eyed the door speculatively. 'Next up, he'll probably want to carry Petra over the threshold.'

Nathan was beginning to enter into the spirit of things now. 'So practically speaking…he'll be holding Petra and he'll have to get the key card in the door…and he has a dodgy knee.'

'Exactly and I have no idea how easy it would be without the knee issue.' She hesitated. 'Did you…?'

'Carry Alexis over the threshold? No, I didn't.' He could hear the terseness in his voice, but had no wish to elaborate. He'd messed up, had got the honeymoon surprise completely wrong. And he didn't want that to happen to Greg and Petra.

Poppy glanced at him and sighed. 'Bother. I was hoping you'd be able to advise based on experience. OK, we'll have to use our common sense. I wouldn't normally worry, but with his knee…'

'I know.' And he did. Knew how sensitive his friend was about his knee, how much he hated being 'less of a man', hated to think there were things he couldn't do any more that he could do so easily before the accident. 'Look, why don't we try it?'

'What do you mean?'

'I'll carry you over the threshold. See how it feels to go in blind, not knowing if the door pushes in or pulls out, how easy the key card is to manoeuvre.' It was a good idea and one he wouldn't have any issues with if it weren't Poppy he was picking up. But he wouldn't let foolish attraction get in the way of the job at hand.

She bit her lip and then nodded. 'If you don't mind, that's probably a good plan. But I'll pop downstairs first and put some high heels on so we can gauge the width of the door better.'

A few minutes later she returned, clad now in a pair of stilettos and a bulky coat.

'I know I look ridiculous but I thought the coat would add a bit of weight and make the whole thing a little trickier—to mirror a complicated dress.'

Yet somehow she didn't look ridiculous and once again he marvelled at her ability to pull off clothes that would have looked silly on anyone else.

'I'm ready. Shall we start from the lift?' Her voice was surely a touch higher, a tad more breathless than usual as she stood outside the lift.

Oh, Lord. This was a bad, bad idea, but somehow he had to do it and there was no point overthinking or it would become awkward. So he had to ignore what his insides were doing, ignore the cartwheels going on in his stomach at the idea of her proximity and get on with it.

In one swift movement Nathan scooped her up into his arms and his pulse rate accelerated as the now, oh, so familiar smell of shampoo assailed him. He bit back a groan as she wriggled slightly, her body so warm, so enticing, and then she placed her arms around his neck.

'Right.' He started to walk, focused on counting the steps to distract himself from the rush of sensation, to prevent him from leaning down and brushing his lips against hers…four, five, six. 'So here's the door. And the key would be in my pocket.'

'OK. So this would be where realistically Petra would have to get the key out of his pocket.'

She slipped one hand down and put it in his back pocket and he heard her muffled gasp. 'Sorry, sorry, sorry. Um… Oh, God, I've nearly dropped it. No, I'm good. I have it. Um…'

He saw the flush creep up her cheeks and he couldn't help it, he laughed. Somehow it felt foolish to pretend they weren't struggling with this, both reacting to each other on an elemental level. 'Feeling the heat?' he asked, and he couldn't hold back a grin as she rolled her eyes at him.

'Don't flatter yourself,' she retorted.

'So it's nothing to do with my…?'

'No, it isn't. Just get on with it. And stop smirking.'

In a slow deliberate movement she put both arms back around his neck, wriggled her body and suddenly all inclination to smirk left him. She placed a hand on his cheek. 'You sure you're not feeling the heat?' she asked softly, her voice low and teasing.

'OK… OK. You've made your point. The heat

exists—now we have to ignore it.' It occurred to him that as a fire strategy the strategy sucked—if you ignored the flames you got burnt.

He manoeuvred the key into the door and then pushed the door open with his back and carefully swung round.

'That was an easy fit through the door.'

'I'll put you down now.' He braced himself as she slid down him, took his arm to steady herself as she balanced on the heels and hurriedly turned away from him, her face still flushed, her speech rapid.

'Good, so we've established the threshold carrying is possible. Now let's assess the suite itself. I've gone for the deluxe larger one over the small, more cosy one. I think however in love you are a bit of space is nice. So what do we think of the décor?'

'Nice. Clean. Nothing that could annoy anyone but it's not impersonal either.' Walls a cool neutral colour, the pictures tasteful but with a bit of colour, and a theme of wood gave the room a clean, welcoming aura. The wooden floors were comfortable underfoot and the furniture was simple but functional.

She slipped out of the coat, placed it on a chair. 'Right, we need to test the bed…sorry. That was a silly thing to say. I'm a bit…on edge.' A blush crept over her cheeks.

'I get it. Me too.'

They both stood contemplating the massive wooden four-poster, the posts simply carved, the canopy cool and luxurious.

'It…it looks comfortable,' he offered, a hint of desperation in his voice. 'Which is pretty important for a couple on their honeymoon.'

'Though it's more important it *feels* comfortable.' She walked over to the bed, placed both hands on the mattress and pressed down and up and he came and did the same on his side. Both looking away from the other, up at the ceiling, out of the window, anywhere but at each other.

'This is ridiculous,' she said eventually. 'We are like a couple of teenagers, embarrassed by a bed.'

'The worst of it is when we were teenagers we couldn't have cared less.'

'Do you think that's odd? That back then we really were oblivious to attraction and now… it's making us behave like adolescents?'

As she spoke she sat on the bed, her back against the headboard, and he followed suit.

'I think back then we needed our friendship too much to risk jeopardising it in any way.'

She considered and then nodded. 'Yup. I think you're right. I would never have sacrificed our friendship on the altar of a relationship. After all, I knew relationships didn't last.'

'You were out of my league anyway. I was a geek with a convict for a father. You were beautiful and intelligent and talented and…rich.'

'That was never how I saw you. I mean, we never really spoke about parents, yours or mine. You were just my friend, the boy who would stand up to bullies but was scared of spiders.'

He glanced up at the ceiling. 'No spiders in sight. Thank goodness.'

'Don't worry, I'd rescue you.' She turned, her face lit in a reminiscent smile. 'Like I did all those years ago. Do you remember?'

'How could I forget? Having to confess a fear of spiders would be etched on any young man's memory.'

She grinned. 'I wouldn't call it a confession. More of a revelation. I heard you screech…'

'A manly yell, as I recall.'

'Then I came running through to see you. You were literally paler than milk. But you told me not to worry, you'd save me.'

'And I would have. If you hadn't leapt in and rescued me, I'd have wrestled that monster spider to the ground.'

Poppy snorted with laughter and he felt a funny glow in his chest, a warmth that he hadn't felt for a very long time. 'It was not a monster. It was tiny.'

'Nope. It was gigantic, gargantuan.'

'Well, lucky I was there. For the spider's sake. Poor thing. I'm sure he was shivering in his boots with fear when I caught him and freed him.'

'I can remember how awestruck I was that you were so fearless. I'm guessing you were less than awestruck.'

'Actually it was kind of endearing and... It reminded me of—' She broke off.

'Reminded you of...?' he prompted, saw the smile fade from her face.

'Michael,' she said finally. 'He was scared of spiders too.'

'I didn't know that.' He hesitated. 'How is Michael?' Her half brother had been the only member of her family Poppy had ever really discussed at all, the one she'd been in contact with. The only member of her family he'd ever met, albeit briefly when Michael had come to pick Poppy up.

'I don't really know.' She shrugged. 'I don't want to talk about it. I screwed up and now... now I don't really know how to fix it.'

'You sure you don't want to talk about it?'

'I'm sure.' Her voice was tight. 'We never really talked about family much anyway, did we?'

'No, I guess we didn't.' Until now. After all, last night Poppy had confided in him, shared the details of her relationship with her mother.

The memory renewed the sense of anger he felt for the crass stupidity of Honor Carruci. And now, now it sounded as though Poppy had lost the one person of her family worth knowing. 'But that doesn't mean we can't now,' he said. 'The offer's there if you want it.'

'Thank you. And the same goes for you.' The words were gentle but held a hint of a question, an invitation to open up here and now, and he was almost tempted. Almost. But how could he? How could he share things with Poppy that he had shared with no one, not even Alexis?

The realisation, the name, were a jolt, causing him to question what he was doing. Sitting on a bed, laughing, talking, feeling warm and happy. With Poppy. The woman his wife had felt threatened by. His wife. Alexis. The woman he'd let down in life. Hell, he hadn't even realised she'd felt threatened, hadn't realised that Poppy had left their friendship for his sake.

Nathan closed his eyes. This wasn't Poppy's fault. It was his.

'I'll bear it in mind,' he said, trying to keep his voice light, all too aware of her green eyes resting on him with a fleck of concern, a glint of compassion.

'Good. You OK?'

And even now as he looked at her, the urge to lean forward and kiss her was nigh on overwhelming, but he knew that if he did there was no way they would be able to stop it from spiralling and here there would be no handy distraction from a fallen bottle. Here there was just the cool expanse of clean silken sheets and a four-poster bed.

And so he forced himself backwards, pressed his back against the wooden headboard. 'I'm good. So what's next on the agenda for the day?'

She studied him and then swung her legs over the bed. 'I think it's time for something from my list of venues for after the ceremony. Let's check out the funfair.' She gave him a quick smile. 'Have some fun.'

CHAPTER NINE

FUN. POPPY MUSED on the concept as they made their way towards the park where the funfair was located. Who would have thought a week ago that this could be happening?

'So what do multimillionaire CEOs do for fun?' she asked. 'When was the last time you had fun? Real fun?'

He slowed down and his forehead creased in thought. 'The time Greg and I test-drove the first model of the Envii—that was fun.'

'That does sound like fun, more than fun. But I'm talking about non-work-related fun. What do you do when you're not working?'

There was a silence as he thought, as they approached the funfair, lit up in the evening dusk, and Poppy gave a small cry of delight. 'It's beautiful,' she said as she absorbed the twinkling illumination of the fairy lights, sprinkled in the trees and showcasing the height and depth of the rides and kiosks that made up the fair.

'It is,' he agreed.

She glanced at him, saw that he had a slight frown on his forehead. 'Well, when you've worked out the answer to my question let me know. But in the meantime it sounds to me like you are overdue some good old-fashioned fun.' She saw the expression on his face, not guilt exactly but something akin to it, and she rolled her eyes. 'Think of it as work-related if you like,' she said. 'We're doing this for the proposal.'

'How so?' he asked as they wandered through the rides, saw smiling children, heard the screams of excitement from the more daring of the rides.

'I thought about what you said at breakfast, about not recreating anything from Greg's past life. But I do still want to jazz the whole thing up. So this is my new idea. Why not have the ceremony and then they can come and have some fun here? No-pressure fun, that does still build adrenalin but without any competition or stress to his leg. There are loads of really nice restaurants, so there could be a lovely reception sit-down dinner, after going on some of the rides. What do you think?'

'I think that that is an amazing idea.' He studied her face. 'And it shows me how much you listen and care and that's why you are a very good wedding planner.'

'Why, thank you, sir.' The praise warmed her, gave her an unaccustomed glow of confidence. 'Now, where shall we start?'

He grinned at her and something twisted inside her. The smile made him look boyish and almost carefree, and she sensed he'd made some sort of decision. 'As someone who has officially forgotten how to have fun, I put myself in your hands.'

'You do? Perfect. There is a wooden roller coaster here that is one hundred years old. Or there's a ride, which sounds utterly terrifying. You go up to a massive height and then literally vertical drop. Maybe I'll do the baby version of it, which apparently three years olds can do! And there's a Ferris wheel.' She came to a stop. 'So what first?'

'The roller coaster,' he said promptly.

As they climbed into the red seat of the roller coaster she was suddenly, oh, so aware of him, the strength of his thigh next to hers, the sense of exhilaration not only due to the impending ride. A ride that coasted and swooped them along the wooden tracks, never terrifying, though the sudden drops caused her to cry out as her tummy looped the loop, and the momentum pushed her body willy-nilly against his.

'I loved that,' she said as they disembarked. 'My level of speed and risk. Your choice next.'

He hesitated. 'Let's try the Tik Tak next. It's a flat ride and the pods spin round in loads of different directions.'

Poppy looked up at him, and by now adrenalin and the sheer hormonal thrill of being in such proximity to Nathan had clearly made her take leave of her senses. 'No, let's do the intense roller coaster.'

'You sure?'

'Yes.' Because she knew he wanted to, knew he'd picked the relatively tame Tik-Tak because it was flat and in her comfort zone. 'I'm sure. Sometimes it's good to try scary things, right?'

'Right.'

But somehow as they walked, dodging the balloon sellers toting an assortment of bright helium balloons, and inhaling the scents of candy floss and the sizzle of burgers, she felt as though she meant more than just a roller coaster. This, all this, whatever it was with Nathan, was scary too. Or at least edging her out of her comfort zone.

Nerves kicked in as they joined the queue and she looked up at the looping, massive expanse of roller coaster, heard the screeches and yells of the people riding it.

'It says it exposes you to up to four G, which is more than a space shuttle during launch. I don't even know what that means.'

'G Force,' he said. 'It's a way to measure acceleration. So one G is the acceleration we feel due to the force of gravity. That's why our feet stay on the ground and why they don't in space. On a roller coaster when you drop, it is G force that pushes you back against the seat.'

'I'm not sure if that makes me feel more nervous or less.'

'You don't have to do this.' His gaze was steady as he looked into her eyes. 'You've got nothing to prove.'

'I know. I want to do it.' And if that wasn't one hundred per cent true it was true enough.

'OK. Let's go.'

Once they were strapped in, he took her hand in his. 'Hold on tight. I won't let go.'

She nodded, her stomach twisting as the ride started, gained speed, whirled, looped, screeched, somersaulted and raced along the tracks. And as the wind caught her hair, and her stomach lurched, she heard herself screaming in exhilaration and through it all she was aware that their hands were intertwined even as they raised them in the air along with everyone else.

Once it was over she disembarked and he took her hand again. 'That was utterly terrifying— But I loved it. I'm not sure I'd do it again, but I loved it.' She smiled up at him and caught her breath at the look in his eyes. Pride mixed with warmth. 'Right, what next?'

'How about the ride that takes us through the Hans Christian Andersen stories?'

'OK. That is a must-see.' She looked up at him and smiled.

They reached the ride and soon they were in the trunk that was going to carry them through the array of figures that retold the celebrated fables, each one voice-overed, and for the duration Poppy lost herself in the fictional tales until they emerged back into the illuminated evening of Copenhagen.

'That was very well done,' Nathan said. 'The way they have made it appeal to both kids and adults.'

'Yes.' An image popped into her head. Nathan and herself sitting not in one trunk but two and with them were a couple of kids, a red-haired little boy and a blonde girl, chattering and laughing, absorbed by the stories unfolding.

Whoa. OK. She was letting the atmosphere, the illusions, the stories mess with her head. Yes, they were having fun, but as part of a research into a work proposal.

'So what do you think? Will Greg and Petra like it?'

'What's not to like? I think you've nailed this part of it.'

'Then how about we celebrate with a hot dog? I think they are trialling a vegan option.'

'You don't have to go vegan just for me.'

'I know. But I want to. I'd like to help, but also I'm interested in the taste.'

'You are?'

'Yes. So if you want to discuss taste and texture and tell me about your breakthrough moment, I'm more than happy to help.'

'I appreciate that. You wait here and I'll go and grab the food. I'll be back in a minute.'

As Nathan walked back towards Poppy, two vegan dawgs slathered in ketchup, mayonnaise and mustard in his hand alongside a plain one for research purposes, he looked down at his feet. He felt different, lighter, as though he were floating, as if something heavy had dissolved.

Which was obviously ridiculous. There was a scientific reason behind all of this. Something to do with adrenalin, and food and atmosphere and the fact he hadn't had fun for a long time. But it was nothing to do with Poppy. At all.

Yet when he saw her, saw her face light up as she saw the hot dogs, saw her hair dishevelled now after the rides, recalled her look of absorption as they'd watched the stories, the feel of her hand clutching his on the roller coaster, something twisted in his chest.

He sat down next to her. 'OK. Taste and tell me.'

She bit into the hot dog, her face focused, a small frown of concentration on her face. 'OK, so the texture is really similar and that's the main thing, really, I think. Because once you cover it in the condiments that's of primary importance.'

He nodded. 'Agreed. Texture is important and so is aftertaste and…'

'And so is familiarity,' she said thoughtfully. 'Because there is an expectation, isn't there, when you eat a hot dog at a fair?'

Nathan looked at her, struck by the observation.

'Because,' she continued, 'it's evocative. I'm eating this and the taste, the tang of ketchup, the softness of the roll, it's brought back a memory. A childhood memory.' She shook her head, almost in wonder. 'It's strange how a taste can bring something back so vividly.'

'Tell me.'

'I think my dad was between girlfriends and wives and he decided to take Sylvia and me out. Michael must have been with his mum. So it was just the three of us. I was over the moon, completely over the moon. It wasn't often I was included. We went bowling and it turned out I had a natural talent and I was showing off like mad. I wanted to impress Dad and then I realised what would make him happiest. I saw his face when Sylvia was losing and he looked mad so I let Sylvia win.'

'That was kind of you.'

'It really wasn't.' She grinned. 'I'm sorry to say it was utterly selfish. I wanted to be asked on another trip out, wanted another family day, and I figured the best way forward was to give Sylvia the limelight. I already understood she was the important one, Dad called her his "fashion princess" and I think I already understood on some level that he planned to leave his business to her. It was part of our family story and I accepted it without thought.'

He looked for bitterness in her face, but could find none.

'Anyway, after bowling we had hot dogs. Covered in ketchup. And my dad put mayo and mustard on mine and I'd never tried that before and it made me feel happy that the three Winchesters were eating the same food, had the same tastes. I felt like Sylvia must feel all the time.'

Nathan looked at her. 'It must have been hard, knowing that Sylvia was the favoured one.'

'It was and it wasn't. It's hard to explain really. It's the way it was and I suppose both Michael and I were OK with it because we remembered Sylvia's mum and she had always been kind to us. It was harder for Michael really. Because back then everyone thought I'd be inheriting on my mum's side, so it was Michael who would get nothing.'

She stopped speaking and for an instant she checked, the hot dog halfway to her mouth. 'Anyway, after the hotdogs we had ice-cream sundaes and—'

'Whoa. Hold on a minute.' His brain reran her words. 'What do you mean, "back then"?'

'Back then was what we were talking about, how we all felt back then.' She spoke quickly, placed her hot dog down, wiped her fingers, raised a hand to touch a tendril of hair, dropped it.

'Nope. That is not the context. The way you said back then implies that was then and something is different now.' He waited but she said nothing, the silence now awkward, and he sensed she was trying to decide what to do, what to say, realised he was holding his breath.

'Poppy. Earlier when I said if you want to talk, then let's talk, I meant it. I'm happy to listen, maybe I can help you. I'd like to.' The words were true; he did want to help.

'OK. It's no big deal, I suppose. And I told

you half the story already, why not share the whole thing?' The off-hand tone was clearly contrived. 'My mum has decided that she wants to leave her share of the business to only her kids with Don, not me.'

'Say what now? Why would she do that? *Can* she even do that?' Outrage started to build inside him.

'Apparently so. She says the three of them will work well together as a team and she will be offering them all roles in the company.'

'You can fight that, surely. You are as entitled to a share as they are.'

'I don't want to fight. I didn't know my grandparents—it was their empire and now it is my mum's and so she should do with it as she wishes. And this is her wish. It's not surprising really, is it? I told you she'd like to erase the past, pretend her first marriage didn't happen. Now she's done the final severance.'

'But…' Words failed him. 'That is blatantly, horribly unfair. And not very clever either—she's losing your talent.'

'She doesn't think I'm talented. Which is fine. There is no reason why I should be entitled to a job on a plate.'

'Actually, yes, there is. You are entitled by virtue of your birth and if you aren't entitled then your half-siblings aren't either.' He shifted on the bench so he was looking at her properly, tried to fathom why she would accept this without a fight. 'Is that why you decided to give up on fashion?'

'Yes. It seemed like time to make a break as well. Put fashion and my mum behind me. Accept she really does not want me in her life in any way, shape or form. Accept too that I don't necessarily have what it takes.'

'So you want to give up your birthright?'

'Yes. What else can I do?'

'Talk to your siblings. On both sides. Maybe they will talk to your mum or dad, get them to see how unfair this is. You would be an asset to either company.'

She shook her head. 'You don't know that. And it doesn't make any difference anyway. I've put fashion behind me. Star Weddings is my future, or at least I hope it is.' She put the last piece of hot dog in her mouth and rose to her feet. 'Time for the Ferris wheel, I think.'

Her tone was final and after a momentary hesitation he nodded. 'Sure.'

They walked to the massive brightly lit wheel, queued, buckled in, and the wheel began its slow circular turn, the chair rocking slightly from the momentum, the view changing their perspective as they headed skyward. He could feel her pain and his mind whirred as he tried to process the conundrum Poppy had presented him with. Because whilst he didn't doubt the truth of the words, had seen how good she was at her job and admired how she was fighting to keep the company alive, it seemed inconceivable to him that the Poppy he remembered could have abandoned that innate love of fashion. How many times had he seen her, pencil and paper in hand, curled up on a sofa, sitting at a desk, sketching dresses, trousers, outfits, shoes…?

The image was so vividly clear it jogged something, made him think of something more recent. The Poppy of this morning—he'd knocked on the door, gone in, she'd been at the desk, pencil in hand, the same dreamy focus on her face. 'That's what you were doing this morning,' he exclaimed.

'Sorry?' She looked at him, clearly startled. 'We're at the top of the Ferris wheel and that's what you have to say?'

'Yes,' he said simply. 'This morning. The incriminating evidence—you were sketching something. Something to do with fashion.' He sighed, looked round and down. 'I absolutely acknowledge it's stunning, incredibly romantic. The lights, the city, the moonlight. It's all genuinely magical. Now, am I right? About this morning?'

'Does it really matter?'

'Yes.'

'Why? Why does this matter to you?' She turned to him, her red hair glinting. Her eyes held both sadness and challenge. 'In a few days' time we are going our separate ways.'

The question threw him. Poppy was right, and he could feel an incipient dart of guilt, hear an echo of Alexis's voice, probing, asking the same question.

'Why does it matter so much to you when I didn't? When my worries and traumas didn't matter?'

He pushed the query, pushed the voice away. Perhaps it was wrong of him, but just because he had been a bad husband didn't mean he should turn his back on Poppy here and now.

'You're right. In a few days we will go our separate ways but right here, right now, it does matter to me. And surely right here, right now is what matters. I want to help. I want to understand. I want to know.' He gentled his voice. 'If you want to tell me. Here and now. Sitting up looking over Copenhagen.'

She shrugged, an elegant lift of her shoulders, dismissive, though he could sense the wariness, the tension in her body. 'OK. It's no big deal, but yes, sometimes I make a few sketches.'

'So if it's no big deal you won't mind showing

them to me.' He kept his voice low and smooth, watched her face, saw her eyes dart down to the sling bag resting on her lap, realised. 'You've got them with you.'

'I… Oh, for Pete's sake.'

'You'd make a terrible spy. And I would clearly make an amazing detective. Will you show me?' He looked at her and now neither of them was looking at the view, both completely focused on the conversation at hand. 'I can see that it is a big deal and I am not asking lightly. But I'd love to see them.'

And he wondered what had happened to change Poppy. The Poppy of the past had happily sketched away, shown him everything she'd drawn, never hidden her ideas, her talents under a bushel, or a laptop for that matter.

'I don't know.'

'Why not? I'm a safe person to show. I'll be honest, I have no axe to grind and whatever I say after a few days I'll be gone from your life.' The additional reminder jarred. The idea of Poppy not being there, the idea this could be his last chance to see her sketches, sat uneasily and alarm bells started to ring at the back of his head. He pushed them away, refused to be distracted—this was about Poppy.

'So you want to see them now?'

'Yes.'

Slowly, oh, so slowly, she reached into her bag, pulled out a slimline sketchbook and handed it over.

CHAPTER TEN

POPPY TRIED TO focus on the view, on the motion of the Ferris wheel, the brightly coloured balloons above her head, but all she could hear was the rustle of the pages as Nathan turned them. Why on earth had she shown him? Because he was right—he had no axe to grind and she did trust him to give an honest opinion. An opinion she cared about from a man who cared. Another page turned. Focus on the dusky blue of the sky. Because he did care—she'd seen his outrage at her mum's actions, his frustration that she wouldn't fight. And another rustle. Too much caring going on. She could not, would not, start caring for Nathan. He'd made it more than clear they were going separate ways.

The Ferris wheel lurched to a stop and he closed the book and now the butterflies returned with a vengeance as they disembarked, walked away towards the bench they had recently vacated.

She made an attempt at nonchalance. 'So what's the verdict? It's fine if you don't like them.'

'I do like them. I really like them. I more than like them. You are definitely a fashion princess.'

The sincerity in his deep voice warmed her, brought a smile to her lips. 'Really?'

'Really. I'm not an expert but I am a designer, albeit of cars, and I can recognise talent and lines and flair. The big question here is why can't you see it? Why are you questioning your own talent? That's not who you were years ago. Back then you believed in yourself.'

'That was then—maybe it was the arrogance of youth. Or perhaps the belief was in the fact I had a guaranteed place, a position in the world of fashion.' But it was a valid question, one that Poppy hadn't even asked herself. Looking back now to those olden days, she did remember that core of belief. Could almost feel the solid steel of it in her tummy. A core that had somehow been eroded. By facts and by life and by her decision to start anew. Because it was… Easier. Was that really it?

'And now you won't be part of the Carruci empire you don't think you can make it?' There was no judgement in his voice, more a question, and she sensed he was trying to understand. 'Is it because you feel your mother judged you?'

'I don't feel it.' The words a snap, as she re-lived the meetings with her mother. 'I know it. I did try to change her mind, to fight. I told her I believed I'd be an asset to the company, asked for the chance to prove it. Asked for a job the same as she was giving my siblings. I showed her a portfolio of my sketches. Back then I had a real collection, a serious one, not a few sketches. She looked at them, took them, showed them to the board. The verdict was that I wasn't good enough.'

The words had hurt, been a verdict, really, on her as a daughter, a person and a talent. Not good enough. Not as good as Sylvia, not as good as her mother's other children. In that mo-ment she'd understood how Michael must have felt all his life. Not good enough and without an inheritance either.

'Hey.' Nathan's voice was gentle as he took her hand in his, the clasp full of comfort. 'That must have been horrible to hear but, from what you've told me, I don't think you can take your mother's word for anything when it comes to you. She doesn't see you as the person you are. And she's head of the board—if she said she didn't like your sketches, ten to one they'd agree whether they believed it or not. You can't give up because of one person's opinion. Think about authors who get rejected again and again and then turn into bestsellers.'

'Well, I've been rejected by two top fashion leaders, people who head up global fashion brands.'

'Two people who inherited global fashion empires and are emotionally connected to you, have a personal relationship—you cannot trust their judgement. Anyway, did you even show your father your work?'

'No. Because—' She broke off. 'We aren't really talking.'

'There you are. So he isn't going to be objective, is he? Why roll over and give up? Why not prove them wrong? Join a different fashion company, or go it alone.'

'I can't do that.'

'Why not?'

Another valid question. 'Because I'd be banking on my name. People would give me a chance because I'm a Winchester or because of my connections or because it makes a good story.'

'None of that matters—they are just excuses. Even if your name comes into play, that will only hold good for so long. If you don't have the talent it won't work.'

Too many questions swirled inside her. Had she taken the easy way out? No, she hadn't. It wasn't about being easy, it was about being right, it was about protecting herself. Damn it she didn't want to go looking for a job, have the humiliation of the world knowing neither of her parents thought her good enough. Right after the disintegration of her relationship, her father's betrayal, followed by her mother's. Enough had been enough. And, damn it, Nathan should get that.

'It has nothing to do with fear or weakness or giving up.' Though somehow now there was nagging doubt in her mind and she glared at Nathan.

He raised his eyebrows. 'I didn't say it was.'

'But you're thinking it, saying I am making excuses. I'm not. I am happy with my life, I love my job with Star Weddings, I want to save the company I am part of. This is my life now, a clean break from the past.' The injustice of it occurred to her. Here was Nathan trying to make her do something he had no wish to do himself. 'I mean, isn't that exactly what you want, Nathan? A clean break from the past.' A clean break from Poppy. 'To move on as best you can.' From the love of his life. And a sudden sadness hit her.

There was a silence and then she saw the shadows cross his face, closed her eyes. 'Sorry, that was a cheap shot. You are trying to move on from grief and loss and tragedy.'

'It wasn't a cheap shot and I'm sorry to be so pushy. I have no right to do that. What your mum did must have knocked you for six. I of all people get that you want a clean slate, a new start. But all I would say is that you should still believe in your talent. I do.'

His words made her think and she knew they were words to value and treasure. 'Thank you.' She sighed. 'Truly. And now, now I feel that we have forgotten what we should be doing. Having fun.'

'Agreed. And I know exactly what we should do next…how about the bumper cars?'

'It's a plan. And for the next few hours let's focus on the present and enjoying ourselves. You and me.' Because it was clearer to her than ever that there really was no future friendship on the horizon, Nathan had made that more than clear and she felt a sudden need to stop over-thinking, over-analysing. Why not enjoy the here and now and let the future look after itself?

And she sensed Nathan felt the same way as they childishly raced after each other on the bumper cars, crashed into each other with abandon, as they shouted and yelled on the massive vertical drop, where she found herself clutching his hand in sheer terror, found herself remaining hand in hand with him as they circled the

fair. Rode the wooden roller coaster again, went
through the haunted house, ate candy floss and
ice cream and throughout it all they teased each
other, laughed, talked about anything and everything as long as it was trivial. They covered
films, music and books until they came to the
end of the evening and the fireworks display.

As they stood, close to each other in the
crowds, both of them looking up at the flash-
ing explosions, the vivid bursts of colour, Cath-
erine wheeling across the Copenhagen indigo
sky, Poppy knew that she was in danger, danger
of caring, danger of hurt, and yet she couldn't
seem to help herself. The future might hold
pain but surely she couldn't get that hurt, not
over a few more days. After all, she'd walked
away from Nathan once and survived. No reason why she couldn't do the same again. In the
meantime she'd enjoy the fireworks.

Fireworks. Funfairs. Roller coasters. The scent
of smoke, of candy floss, of Poppy's vanilla
shampoo. The shouts of people on rides, Poppy's gasp of terror as an eerie chain-jangling
zombie popped up out of the darkness in the
haunted house. All these images and more jos-
tled in Nathan's brain the following day, as he
walked towards the gardens in the middle of
Copenhagen.

Poppy had gone to sort out the legal technicalities of getting married in Copenhagen, leaving him to his own devices again for the morning. Now he was on his way to meet her to check out an outdoor wedding venue in the park dating back four hundred years and founded by royalty. He glanced down at Poppy's message and headed along the sweep of pathway, aware of a tingle of anticipation at the thought of seeing her. What the hell was going on? He'd seen her a scant couple of hours ago over breakfast, hell, he'd seen her in his dreams as well, and now that insidious guilt started to tendril inside him.

No, he wouldn't make whatever was going on something to feel guilty about, wouldn't tarnish Poppy in any way. All they had done was to have some fun and there was nothing wrong with that. Especially when he'd made it clear that there was no future for them, so surely there could be nothing wrong with having a few days of innocent fun. After all, it had turned out that in some ways they had been cheated of years of potential friendship, so, damn it, somehow, logical or not, he felt the universe and Alexis owed them a few days of friendship.

As if on cue he saw her slender form rise

from a bench and walk towards him and his own pace quickened.

'Hey.'

'Hey.' She looked up at him, her smile tentative. 'Did you have a good morning?'

'Yes. I did. I did try the gym this morning and it was great apart from the fact I nearly gave the person on the treadmill next to me a heart attack. I had a sudden idea for a protein compound. I yelled and then raced out of there to write it down, also terrorising the poor bloke on the reception desk by demanding pen and paper.'

'So a real breakthrough?'

'A possible beginning of one.'

'I'm glad. I've also looked up various vegan places here and I thought we could try to visit a few.'

'Thank you.' A renewed trickle of surprise and warmth ran through him and he had a sudden absurd impulse to take her hand in his. But there had been enough of that last night and here there was no excuse, no reason to do that. He liked how Poppy got involved in his projects; she always had. 'Do you remember how you went and bought me seven different varieties of flour to make white sauces with?'

'Yes, I do. I hadn't even heard of some of them. I found them in that amazing little grocery round the corner from me. And then you did lots of research into flour and we ended up making pakoras with the gram flour.'

She looked up at him with a smile on her lips. 'I can practically taste them now. They were scrumptious.'

And so was she. She looked so pretty, her smile lit up her face and he could remember her back then, dipping the sliced potatoes in the batter, her smile as they tasted the finished product, their high five. And suddenly he got exactly why Alexis had felt threatened, could almost hear his wife's voice.

'You get it, right, Nathan? The two of you were such a...team.'

And he and Alexis hadn't been. He shut down the treacherous thought instantly. They had been different, that was all. Alexis would have preferred a husband who had remained in banking, built that sort of career, safe. She hadn't found the rise of Envii exhilarating, hadn't wanted her banker husband to be side-lining as a welder. And that had been OK. He'd known that about Alexis when he'd married her and he'd loved her.

And he'd failed her.

'Nathan?' Poppy's voice brought him back to the present and he slowed down, realised he'd quickened pace without meaning to. 'Can we slow down? We're meant to be soaking in the atmosphere, checking out the scenery, imagining this as a place to have a wedding.'

'Sorry. I'm on it.'

'Unless you're having another breakthrough moment, in which case forge ahead, stand on your head, whatever you need to do.'

'Nope. I think inspiration has flown for the day.' But her words had lightened his mood. Perspective, that was what he needed, and the knowledge that, whilst Poppy might be unsettling him, soon she would be out of his life. And this was not her fault; she didn't want this attraction and Alexis's feelings had not been provoked in any way deliberately, had no foundation. Back then he and Poppy had not had a single thought of being in a relationship. They had been friends.

And now?

Now they were nothing, or soon would be. And now he needed to think about these gardens as a wedding venue.

They walked on and he tried to focus on the beauty of the surroundings, the ancient grandeur of the massive trees that lined the clear sweep of the paths, casting pools of shade. The bright pops of colour and the scent of the flowers, red, pink and green, that should captivate his eyes as they walked bathed in sunlight.

Then there were the rose arches and the lush green of the lawns dotted with people, tourists and residents. He tried his hardest to take mental notes but somehow his focus always returned to the woman walking next to him.

The way the sun lit the glorious colour of her hair pulled back into a sleek ponytail, the style showcasing the classic contours of her face, the high cheekbones, the straight nose and the sparkling green of her eyes. Her look today was smart casual, simple, yet it had her distinctive style—the russet dungarees over the black T-shirt, the shoes, as always, making an extra statement.

'It's definitely beautiful, romantic and peaceful as a setting,' she said. 'The scent of herbs and flowers, the musical splash and flow of the water from the fountains. It's a welcome contrast to all the legal admin of the morning.'

'How did it go?'

'I'll write it all up for you to check but it's relatively straightforward as long as we pay attention to detail. Make sure they have up to date passports and we get all the right documentation.'

'It sounds like you have it in hand. I will definitely give Petra a glowing report of your efficiency and your commitment.'

'Thank you. I'm worried though as there is

so much choice. They can get married here, or there are other equally beautiful gardens or they could get married at the opera or in the planetarium. We're going to check out as many as we can but I don't want to overwhelm Petra with too much choice. Anyway—' she came to a stop '—this is where the ceremony would take place. Under the pergola there and in the direct line of the castle.'

He looked up at the turreted castle.

'Apparently four hundred years ago King Christian IV first bought the park and then decided it needed a building, so this is what he built. A palace.'

'It's certainly eye-catching.' The red brick wall contrasted with the green and bronze eaves and the Renaissance turreted towers and spires climbed the skyline. 'And complete with surrounding moats.'

'Fairy-tale style. And there is a sense of history as well. And afterwards we could have a picnic and then set off for the funfair. What do you think?'

'I think you've got this sorted and…whatever option they choose it will be a magical day.'

'That's what I want for them, for any couple I plan a wedding for —that, no matter what happens after, they can look back to their wedding as being perfect. Magical and perfect. For them both.' Her look was intent. 'You promise you'll go over this proposal carefully, think of anything I've missed. I mean, the funfair won't be any good if either of them is scared of heights. Or if there's anything that may not occur to them but would spoil the day on the day. And you're sure Greg will enjoy it too?'

'Yes. I promise I will do my job. I want the day to be perfect for them as well—no unintentional mishaps or surprises gone wrong. So I will truly think about it properly.'

She frowned. 'You sound like you're speaking from experience.' She hesitated and asked, 'How was your wedding? I hope it was truly magical. I know I didn't come but I want you to know I thought about you all day and I sent you loads of positive vibes.'

'The ceremony was magical, everything Alexis wanted. Small, cosy, intimate.'

The most important people are you and me, but I want to show you off as well.'

'She'd lost her parents before we met, just before. That's how we met, actually—she was struggling and a tutor asked me to help her out a bit, to catch up.'

'I remember that. Remember you talking about her, before you started dating.'

Nathan looked back; Alexis had been his first girlfriend and she'd seemed so fragile, so sad and he'd wanted to help, to fix things, make her happy, and when he'd realised she liked him romantically he'd been flattered and he'd jumped at the chance because in Alexis he'd seen a path to having a relationship where he could be the man his father hadn't been. A secure, supportive, honest partner, a provider who truly provided.

'Anyway, she didn't have any family and so we kept it to a small group of friends, and had a champagne and cream tea reception. She said it was her perfect day and that made me feel on top of the world. That I'd made a good start to marriage, that I'd be a good husband.' He sighed, caught up now in the past. 'Then it all went a bit wrong.'

'What happened?' Her voice low, she prompted him to continue.

'She'd asked me to arrange the honeymoon, surprise her. She trusted me and I got it wrong.' He could still recall the bitter sear of self-recrimination in his younger self, the fear that he'd spoilt it all, that he was in fact like his father, a bad husband. He shook his head now. 'God knows what I was thinking. I booked a romantic isolated cabin in the woods, when of course I should have known Alexis would want five-star luxury.'

'Anyone can make a mistake and I bet the

cabin you picked was the very best one you could find.'

'It was but it was still a cabin in the woods. That's why I didn't carry Alexis over the threshold—by the time we got there it was pretty clear I'd messed up.'

Poppy opened her mouth as if she was going to say something and he pre-empted her. 'It was fair enough, Poppy. I don't think Alexis could have been nice about it—it really showed I hadn't picked up on a single hint she'd dropped in the weeks before.'

'I was going to say I don't blame her.' She gave a quick smile. 'Though, yes, you're right. I do feel defensive on your behalf. But I was going to ask why you picked the cabin. You're not really a woods sort of person and what about the spiders?'

'I thought she'd like it.' Even now he didn't understand what he'd been thinking. 'I thought she'd rather it was the two of us. Because she'd said that so many times, how much she preferred being with just me to being in groups. Anyway, I sorted it out; we sat down together and Alexis chose the hotel she'd actually been hoping I'd surprise her with. I managed to get a last-minute reservation and we packed up and set off to the hotel the next day. So the situation was saved.'

She studied his face. 'You still feel bad, don't you?'

'A little bit. It's like you said—you should be able to look back to your wedding day and it should be perfect. Alexis couldn't.'

'Actually, from Alexis's viewpoint I don't see the problem.'

'What do you mean?'

'She knows you chose the cabin with love because you thought it was what she wanted, not because it was what you wanted and you expected her to comply. Then when you realised it wasn't what she wanted you immediately asked her what she did want. And you made it happen. If anything, that adds to the memory in a good way. So don't beat yourself up.' She stepped forward. 'Got it?'

Her serious expression touched him, even as he knew he saw her scrutiny, didn't want her to see too much. His guilt went so much deeper than she could know, based on so much more than that first mistake. That mistake sometimes now felt like an omen he should have learnt from.

The ping of his phone interrupted them and he looked down then back up at her expression, kind and compassionate with the hint of a question. 'Aha,' he said.

'Aha?'

'Yes. Wait here. I have a surprise for you. I'll be back in a minute.'

CHAPTER ELEVEN

POPPY STOOD AND WAITED, curiosity about what Nathan was up to mingled with warmth that he wanted to surprise her. Even as she considered their conversation, wondering why he had been so hard on himself. Perhaps because each 'mistake' felt magnified in the grief over his loss. He had loved his wife and he clearly wasn't over her death. A fact Poppy had to remember. She could not, would not, let herself fall for Nathan.

And here he was… She squinted slightly to try and see what he was doing and then she walked towards him, a slightly puzzled smile on her lips, saw the tentative upturn of his lips.

'Surprise.'

'It's a bike.'

'Well done,' he said kindly, and she grinned.

'Ha-ha. But… I can't ride a bike. I told you that.'

'I know. So I'm going to teach you.' A pause. 'If you want, that is?'

'I'd love that.' Warmth touched her that he'd registered her comment at breakfast the previous day, must have seen the regret, the emotion she'd tried to hide.

'Good. We can do a lesson a day and by the time we leave you will be able to ride a bike.'

She blinked, knew it was ridiculous to feel tearful, but she did. She hauled in a breath. 'Your farewell gift.' A reminder to herself. 'I like it. If you think I can do it. I mean, I have never ridden a bike.'

'You'll be fine.' His deep voice resonated confidence. 'A natural. You're graceful, poised… It'll be a doddle. Especially with my expertise to guide you.'

'So you're not only a scientist, a billionaire CEO and a welder, you also teach cycling on the side.'

'Nope. You are my first pupil but I have faith in my research and my ability. So.' He held the bike steady. 'If you climb on so I can check the saddle is right. You need to be able to touch your feet on the ground. Then I'll remove the pedals so you can learn how to balance. I've checked the Internet and I am pretty sure I've figured out a bike-teaching strategy. Plus this bit of the park is good. Short grass so you can ride on it and if you do fall you won't hurt yourself too much, And a slight slope because that'll be easier to practise gliding.'

Carefully she swung her leg over and sat, couldn't help but smile at him as warmth touched her again at his gesture. And there it was like a bolt sent on the sweet-flower-laden breeze, a sudden awareness of his proximity, his scent a kind of woodsy, clean, masculine smell, and she felt almost dizzy with a longing. A yearning that it could all be different, that somehow she and Nathan could be two people without baggage or a past, two people open to... To what? Love? A future? Her eyes snapped open as she registered the sheer foolish futility of her thoughts.

Between them she and Nathan had enough baggage to sink the *Titanic* if it hadn't hit an iceberg. More than that, she would never willingly put herself in the deliberate path of probable pain and humiliation again.

'What are you doing?' she asked, her voice a small squeak.

'Checking and then I'll remove the pedals. That way you can use it like a balance bike to start with.'

'Sounds good,' she managed as she tried to rein her hormones back into control.

But she watched him, crouched now on the ground so she could see the powerful muscles of his thighs flex, and then he stood up, right next to her, his hands on the handlebars so close to her she thought she'd combust.

And it wasn't only her, she realised—it wasn't. She saw his jaw clench, saw his fingers tighten around the handlebars. And she was tempted, oh, so tempted, to simply pretend to wobble, 'lose' her balance and tumble into him and then he'd catch her in his arms and… and he'd kiss her and she'd kiss him and…that way lay disaster. Absolute disaster. He would be horrified—that was what would happen— and that horror would etch his face. Or would it? He wanted to kiss her—she was sure of it. Only he didn't. Because it would be disloyal to Alexis.

'So what now?' she asked.

There was a pause, and in that pause she saw the desire in his eyes, saw that he too was fighting the attraction. Could swear she heard the whisper under his breath. *Jeez, Larrimore. Don't answer that. Ignore it.'* Wondered what he wanted to say.

Then he managed a smile and his words when he spoke them exuded a heartiness that was surely fake.

'Practice. That's it. Practise getting on and off the bike—I want you to feel comfortable with it, so on and off. Use the brakes and then it won't wobble. Then we'll push the bike to a bit I found earlier.'

Once they'd reached the designated spot, he nodded. 'Right, now let's glide. You need to push off, use your feet to begin with but then gradually try to keep your feet off the ground so you are gliding, but controlling the glide.'

Poppy focused, revelled in the movement, the idea she was figuring it out, the bike picking up speed as she grew in confidence.

'That's it. Use your sense of balance, keep your body even, try going down the slope, keep your feet off the ground. Brilliant.'

The smile on his face, his obvious pride in her achievement, made her smile back and as she did so the frisson of desire grew, a desire that seemed to grow even more as she looked at him, as he jogged alongside her offering encouragement, as exhilaration heightened.

'Keep going, you're doing great.'

'Thank you,' she said as she came to the bottom of the slope, pulled on the brakes. 'I've got a great teacher.'

'I think this is down to you—you're a natural. You're getting it quicker than I did as a child. I insisted on keeping my stabilisers on for ages.'

'Then what happened?'

She climbed off the bike and started pushing back up the slope as they talked.

He hesitated, his voice a little stilted. 'My dad decided it was time.'

'Tell me,' she said softly, hardly able to believe that he'd even mentioned his dad.

'I must have been seven and actually I'd hung onto my stabilisers so long because I really wanted my dad to teach me how to ride without them. It wasn't really Mum's thing and he'd promised he would. Usually he was never around much at weekends—he was always working. But that Saturday he put the paper down and said, "OK, Nate. Today's the day."'

The memory was clearly so real in Nathan's mind and as he recounted it Poppy could picture the small boy he'd been, so excited and happy to be out with his dad.

'He took the stabilisers off and held onto the back and told me to pedal. But I wouldn't unless he promised to hold on. And he promised. "I won't let go," he said. But of course he did; I heard him shout, "You're doing it, you're doing it, Nate," and I realised he'd let go. And I was doing it, riding on my own and it felt great, but it also felt terrifying, like I was going further and further away from my dad. Because he'd let go.'

'But you could ride your bike.'

'And I was ecstatic. I can still remember the sheer joy and sense of pride. I can still taste the chocolate-chip ice cream I had to celebrate, the sweetness and the cold and looking at my bike leant against a chair because it didn't have stabilisers any more. And my dad ruffling my hair and saying he was proud of me.' His smile was one of reminiscence.

'That's a good memory,' she said. Hesitated. 'I'm glad you have some good memories.'

But that was the wrong thing to say; she could see it by the set of his lips, the smile erased as he shook his head as though he were shaking the memory away.

'What's wrong?'

'Nothing.' His voice was tight. 'Let's keep going.'

'No.' She came to a stop, leant the bike against a tree and turned to him. 'I didn't mean to spoil that memory for you. It's important to you and…'

'You didn't spoil it.'

'Well, something did and I'm the only person in the vicinity.' She knew this was important, could see the pain that shadowed his grey eyes and she wanted to help, wanted to ease that hurt. 'Look. Yesterday at the funfair, when I remembered that day with my dad, that was an important memory to me, because of its rarity value. It was still a good memory even though I know it doesn't change all the other things my dad did, the less good things.'

'That's different.' Now there was a snap of anger in his voice. 'Your memory is real...a rare good moment. My childhood memories, those "happy" childhood memories—I don't revisit them because they aren't real.'

'I don't understand. Whatever happened afterwards, those memories are real and precious.'

'Only they aren't. Because that man, he wasn't the man I thought he was, wasn't the man my mum thought he was. You know that. Everyone knows that. All the time he was being a family man, he was also committing fraud, salting away other people's cash. Maybe to him they were just numbers on a spreadsheet, but he must have known what he was doing. Known it was wrong.'

'But...' she started.

'There are no buts. For years I thought my dad was innocent—all through his trial, all through his time in prison, that's what I thought. Because I believed in him—believed in the man who taught me to ride a bike. The man who held my hand as I balanced on a wall when we went for a walk, the man who threw me up in the air and always caught me. I couldn't believe that that man who I idolised and loved, the Dad from my memories, could ever have swindled and conned so many people. Cheated and lied. So I was sure he'd clear his name, sure he wouldn't be convicted. Even when he went to prison I still thought there must have been a mistake somewhere. Because how could my dad, that man, be guilty?'

Poppy bit her lip, knew she mustn't cry, not now, yet her heart wrenched at the pain and raw, sheer confusion Nathan must have endured. She blinked fiercely, reached out and took his hand in hers. 'I wish you'd been right.'

'So do I. But I wasn't. When I was sixteen I decided I would investigate. I was going to prove to the world, the police, the detectives, the financial institutions that my dad was innocent. I found old papers, bank statements, I even went and spoke to the police. A retired officer. And there it was—all in black and white—my father was guilty as charged. No doubt, he wasn't framed, he did it.'

'Do you have any idea why he did it?'

'Gambling. My dad was a gambler on a massive scale. I pieced it all together. I think at first it was a bit of fun, a business day at the races, the odd casino visit. But at some point it stopped being a business event and it became a hobby and then I think he thought he could beat the system, and it became an addiction. And he started to lose—heavily—and then he couldn't keep up the mortgage payments and so he thought he'd "borrow a bit" and so it escalated and escalated until in the end he got careless. Or desperate. I think he was in all sorts of trouble by the end. His debts were eye-watering to say the least. And then he got caught.'

'And your world imploded.'

'It was awful for Mum. Everything we owned was lost. The house, the expensive cars, the bank balance… Everything.'

'And you lost your dad as well.' She looked at him. 'God, Nathan, why didn't you ever tell me any of this?'

'I was twelve when he went to prison. I spent four years convinced he was innocent, reliving all those memories. I was sixteen when I had to face the truth and once I'd faced that I shut those memories down. Blocked my dad from my life and from my thoughts. So when we met at seventeen I'd moved on.'

'Did you see him whilst he was in prison?'

'No. My mum wanted nothing to do with him and he refused to see me. Then once I realised he was truly guilty I didn't want to see him either.'

'And when he came out?'

'It was soon after you left to go travelling. He

wrote me a letter, said sorry, asked for money and that if I gave it to him he wouldn't contact me again. I gave him the money and he has kept his word. I haven't heard from him again.'

'Do you want to?'

He blinked as though the question startled him. 'Absolutely not. I told you—I've accepted who he is and I've moved on. I have nothing to say to him, nothing I want to hear from him.'

'I just wondered if hearing him say sorry, seeing what he has done with his life in the past years may help in some way.' She hesitated. 'I get that he may have turned back to gambling, back to addiction, but maybe he hasn't. Wouldn't you like to know?'

'No. I can't forgive what he did. To me. To my mum. To all those people he cheated. The lies and deceit.'

'I am so sorry, Nathan. I cannot imagine what you went through. And I understand why your childhood memories feel tarnished. Invalid.' And she understood why he'd fought so hard to believe in his dad's innocence. Because that way those memories could be kept, treasured, believed in. She thought, needing to say this right.

'But I believe they are still real, still do have validity. I think whatever else your father was or did, he still loved you. That he wasn't the man you thought he was, but he was still a dad who loved his son and that does mean something. Maybe with you he was the man he wanted to be; there was a part of his life that was good. And he saw you, Nathan, saw his son. My parents never seemed to really see me. That's why I treasure those rare times when they did. Your dad was proud when you rode that bike. That memory is bittersweet but it is also real. And precious.' She paused. 'In my opinion anyway.'

He looked down at her and now she could see the darkness had lightened a little, and he smiled. 'Thank you. Truly. For listening. And for your opinion, your perspective. And, Poppy, I see you. I always did. And you are definitely worth seeing.'

Their gazes held. Now she saw warmth in his, warmth and a spark of desire and so many emotions, and they both froze. So close. And this time…perhaps the conversation, the exhilaration of riding a bike, all the shared confidences, the sharing of a bittersweet childhood memory, she didn't know. But there was a momentum now that couldn't be denied or ignored and she wasn't sure who moved first but then his lips were on hers and she felt the rush of passion, of relief, of rightness. Her earlier fears seemed redundant, forgotten, things to think about at a later date.

She wrapped her arms around his neck, pressed against him and heard his groan as he deepened the kiss, and glorious, tumultuous sensations cascaded through her. She could taste coffee and pastry, felt a gut-clenching need for more and she slipped her hands under his T-shirt, felt the warm, smooth, muscular glide of his back. Her legs trembled with the weight of desire as she lost herself in the sheer glory, the joyousness of him, of Nathan. It felt so ridiculously right and she wanted this, wanted more, her whole body clamouring, yearning, needing what only he could give.

Until the vestiges of consciousness registered the sudden arrival of people, a group of chattering intruders. The advent of reality entered her brain, slowly, too slowly as the need to sustain the kiss tried to foil it. But then she heard a laugh. 'Hey, leave them to it. They're in their own world. Maybe they're on their honeymoon.'

The words burst the bubble; Nathan froze into immobility and then, as the noise of the tourists receded, they disentangled themselves. Now all joy was gone, replaced by a cold sense of dread that now they'd have to face the music, because they'd failed—they'd done exactly what they'd vowed not to do.

His face had settled into cold grim lines, but

more than that she read the shadow of guilt, one she wanted to disperse. He rubbed a hand down his face. 'I don't know what to say. Except I'm sorry. I shouldn't have done that.'

'Hang on, Larrimore. It takes two to tango and I was definitely a willing participant. And, yes, it was a mistake, but that damned pink elephant got too big to ignore—it was all I could see. So, no, *we* shouldn't have done that. But we did and there is no point wallowing in regrets. We can't undo it, but we can make sure it doesn't happen again. And maybe now we've actually done it, that will knock the whole attraction on the head. Goodbye, pink elephant.'

'Do you really believe that?' he asked.

'No. But it sounded good and...' She bit her lip. 'I want it to be true.' Even though it clearly wasn't. Her whole body was still tingling, reverberations clenching her tummy with frustrated desire. 'For both of us.' For him because guilt still shadowed his face. And for her because she couldn't afford to start falling for Nathan and that kiss had felt more than just physical. She stepped towards him. 'We have to put it behind us and we won't repeat the mistake because it's not worth it.' She gave a small smile. 'Even if it was a pretty amazing kiss.'

He nodded once and then again more decisively. 'You're right. We put it behind us. And we do not repeat.' A deep breath and, 'Right. I need to lock the bicycle up. Someone is going to come and pick it up and take it to the hotel for me. Then what's next on the agenda?'

'A visit to the planetarium, but we'll go via the vegan route I mapped out earlier. That way we both get some research done.' She could only hope as they started to walk, careful to keep a massive gap between them, her belated attempt to inject professionalism into the day would work.

Though she knew it wouldn't be that easy. And… She stepped forward, looked up at him. 'And, Nathan. Don't read more into this than there is. It was a kiss. Please don't feel bad.' Only he did, she could see it and the idea made her feel bad, guilty herself, as though they had done something truly wrong rather than misguided.

By tacit consent they started walking.

CHAPTER TWELVE

AND AS THEY walked Nathan tried not to feel bad—he really did. But how could he not? He'd been out of control. Again. Hadn't given anything a thought except Poppy, the need, the desire to kiss her, to have her, to taste her, touch, feel, and even now his skin burned where she'd touched it, his lips still tingled and he still wanted her, damn it. Wanted to kiss her again here and now.

Well, he couldn't. Shouldn't want to.

Alexis's words came back to him. *'You missed Poppy. If she'd hung around would we ever have happened? You wouldn't have wanted me, needed me.'*

The worst of it until now had been that it had been too late to tell Alexis she'd got it wrong. But now the worst had got worse. Because now he wasn't sure if he could tell Alexis that. What if she'd been right?

'Nathan.' Poppy's voice cut in, brittle now,

taut and tight, and he turned, saw her hurry forward to catch up and slowed a pace he hadn't even realised he'd increased. 'You're not looking as though you're forgetting about it. Do not make this more than it was. It was just a kiss.'

'Is that how it felt to you? Just a kiss?'

'It was a special kiss but I'm sure you've kissed other people in the last few years. Without being so devastated.' She closed her eyes. 'Sorry. Not my business.'

'One person. Since Alexis died I've slept with one person. Once. A one-night stand.' Driven more by physical need and a couple of glasses of wine too much. 'She was a nice woman. I didn't know it at the time, but I think she was in a relationship. We were at a business conference abroad, had a few drinks and it just happened. We both went our separate ways after; and she never told anyone and neither did I. But…it didn't feel right. Not because I think there is anything wrong with a one-night stand, but it didn't feel right for me at the time.'

'And did you feel like this after her? Because right now you look ravaged, as though you have done something wrong. You kissed me. One kiss. You slept with someone else.'

'To answer your question, no, I didn't feel guilty. I didn't feel good about myself, but I didn't feel guilt either.'

'Then what's going on?'

Nathan looked around, realised they'd long since left the park behind them. Knew he had to tell Poppy something, could see her frustration, see that his reaction was hurting her.

But he couldn't tell her the full truth, the full story of his marriage to Alexis and what a failure, what a hash he'd made of it. Because that wasn't fair to Alexis—how would she feel about having the words of her diary shared with anyone, let alone Poppy?

Plus it wasn't only about Alexis; there was another element, another facet of his guilt.

'With Diana, the woman at the conference, it wasn't…personal. It was a physical need, a soulless encounter. With you it's personal. We've held hands, laughed, talked, gone down roller coasters, and I could justify that. Could argue that that was OK, that it comes in the realm of friendship, a friendship that we won't continue. But the kiss, that feels wrong because…'

'Because of Alexis?'

'Yes. Because she knew you, was sufficiently threatened by you to ask you to back away from our friendship, was sufficiently worried that I wouldn't agree to that that she went behind my back, never told me what she'd done.' So much so that he'd simply dismissed what she said in her diary as a sick woman's fancy, brought about through sadness that the tragically short life had contained a marriage that had not been good enough, had been full of misery and might-have-beens. And he hadn't known, had been blind to what had been happening under his nose. As his mother had been to his father's other life. Too many parallels, too many things he'd got wrong.

'So kissing me was a betrayal of her?' Her voice was soft and he had no idea what she was thinking.

'That's how it feels to me. But it's more than that. Us, you and me, there can be no future relationship. I don't want a serious relationship with anyone.'

'I know that,' she said. 'So what do you want?'

The question was almost clinical and again he couldn't read a single thought. She was walking, looking straight ahead, her delicate profile unreadable, her tone curious, clinical almost, like a prosecutor questioning a witness. 'I mean, I understand it doesn't feel possible now, but one day in the future, maybe one day you will be able to love again.'

'Not happening.' The words were harsh and as he looked at Poppy, the beauty of her profile, the warmth of her, a sense of panic

touched him. 'That's not what I want. Ever.'
Would never take the risk of navigating those
waters again because he'd end up taking someone else under. The thought of involvement sent
a clammy dread of incipient foretold failure
through him.

'But surely you aren't going to eschew all
relationships for life. I mean, what about attraction? What about sex? You can't want to
be celibate for life.'

'Of course not. But it wouldn't be fair to offer
something I can't give. So I can't offer a woman
marriage, commitment, a family.'

'So you can offer sex, expensive dinners, a
few dates. But nothing…personal.'

'That sounds sleazy.'

'I didn't mean it like that. It's not sleazy. You
could find a woman who is like you, successful in her own right, who doesn't want commitment or family either.'

He looked at her, asked the question he should
have asked at the start of all this. 'Why are we
even having this conversation?'

'Because I hate that kissing me has made
you feel so bad and so guilty. Because it makes
something that felt glorious now feel tawdry.
So I was trying to figure out if it's me or any
woman. I guess I got my answer.'

'Stop. It was not tawdry and it was glorious.

Don't you see? That's why I feel so bad. I enjoyed every moment, every second, every millisecond of our kiss.' Our kiss—that was the problem. Kissing Poppy had been unique and wonderful, it had opened up such a blaze of sensation and feeling and a sense of being alive again after such a long time. And that seemed so unfair to Alexis—of all the women for him to feel this with, Poppy was the worst.

She sighed, a small sigh that combined a wealth of emotion. 'I don't know how I am supposed to feel,' she said honestly. 'But I do believe that Alexis won't grudge you a kiss. She loved you and she knows how much you loved her. You were happy together and if she felt threatened by me at the very start of your relationship, that was understandable. I don't think you need to beat yourself up because we kissed. But I do understand that this, you and me, has no future. And I'm good with that. But we have a couple of days left here—why don't we put the kiss behind us? It's done. We can't undo it. Let's move on. That's what we're good at, isn't it?'

Her tone held resignation and a certain sadness, but also resolution. 'I've got dinner booked at a great restaurant near the funfair and then we're going to a jazz club. Let's concentrate on what we're here to do.'

'Agreed.' Poppy was right. That was the only way forward. Moving on.

CHAPTER THIRTEEN

POPPY HAD NO idea if she was doing the right thing, the wrong thing—wasn't sure, to be honest, what she was doing, what she was trying to achieve. She stared at her reflection in the mirror, saw the glitter in her green eyes, eyes she had emphasised the colour and size of by a careful use of make-up. Freshly washed hair fell in a glossy curtain to her bare shoulders, which were exposed because she'd decided to wear an off-the-shoulder dress.

It was a dress that she'd never worn before and she wasn't sure if she should wear it now. Yes, she loved it, loved the bold red colour, loved the off-the-shoulder design, the slit down the side lined with red ruffles. So of course she should wear it—she'd brought it to Copenhagen to wear, in case she needed to glam up to check out a venue, and now she did. Simple as that.

But it wasn't. Wasn't simple any more at all. When she'd packed the dress she hadn't given attraction factor a thought, hadn't seen it as a dress that would entice, showcase her figure, hadn't seen the slit down the side as being revealing, hadn't pictured Nathan's hands sliding over her bare shoulders, his lips grazing kisses on her shoulder blades.

And Poppy knew that the way you wore clothes changed them, knew she could wear this dress in a less alluring way, could pair it with a shawl, or a jacket that hid the shoulders, altered her body contour. She could wear sensible shoes or she could wear the red, strappy high heels that were eyeing her from the open wardrobe.

Her make-up, the way she walked, the way she talked, all could conspire and complement to attract or show aloofness.

Poppy knew that, knew the choice she was making was deliberate, that she wanted to allure, attract, bedazzle…even if she wasn't sure of her reasoning. But part of it was she didn't buy what Nathan had said earlier.

Years ago, she had accepted Alexis's need for Poppy to exit the stage. Had genuinely believed Alexis was right and so she had stepped aside and she still believed that had been right. Alexis and Nathan had been in love, had had a happy, fulfilled marriage that had been brought short by tragedy. Nathan had clearly loved his wife, wanted her happiness and was devastated by her death. And Alexis had loved her husband, and that love surely meant that she wouldn't want Nathan to give up on relationships, feel this writhe and lash of guilt because he'd kissed Poppy.

Alexis probably hadn't given Poppy another thought for the whole of her marriage and now...well, now Poppy couldn't see the problem with this attraction. She understood why Nathan did, but she thought this time he'd got it wrong. She also accepted that he was entitled to his opinion and Poppy knew she had no right to judge his feelings, his emotions. But she wouldn't deny the attraction any more, wouldn't make this easy for Nathan because she wanted... she wanted...

She looked at her reflection in the mirror and looked away. She didn't want to finish the sentence, didn't know what she wanted, and she hesitated. Instinct told her not to play with fire, that this was foolish, that she should dress in her dowdiest dress, dress down.

Instead she turned away, slipped her feet into the red high heels and headed to the door as Nathan knocked.

She tried to ignore the hammer of her heart as she pulled the door open and saw his mouth literally drop open, saw him step back, and a thrill of power ran through her, balanced only by the knowledge that her own reaction to him was hardly any better. He was wearing a suit, his jacket slung over one shoulder, and he looked utterly gorgeous and all she wanted to do was grab him by his shirt and pull him back into her room.

But she wouldn't. That wasn't her plan—her plan, petty and daft as it sounded, was simply to show him what he was missing. She finally admitted it to herself. Childish but true. But right now she wasn't regretting it, not when she saw the look in his eyes.

'Looking good, Larrimore,' she said, trying to keep her tone light.

'You scrub up pretty well yourself.'

'Then let's go. Dinner first, jazz later.'

As they rode the metro to the restaurant, the silence was surprisingly comfortable yet with an underlay of awareness, as if they were studying each other and trying to decide what to do. She was careful to keep her distance, to not so much as accidentally brush against him, sensed that he was looking at her, trying to gauge her mood.

Well, good luck to him; she had no idea herself, her emotions veering wildly from one sense to another. Almost for something to do she looked down at her phone as it pinged; for a moment she'd thought the tone indicated a message from Bella. But it wasn't, was simply a marketing email. Yet she studied it as if it were of utmost interest, because it gave her something to do. And she thought about her friend, hoped that she was OK, wondered again if she should send her a message, an update.

Now back to Nathan. What was she hoping for here? Nothing. She mustn't hope for anything. There was no future with Nathan—there was a future though. With Bella, with Star Weddings. Quickly, not letting herself think any more, she messaged Bella.

Hey, Bella. I hope it's all going well with you. I wanted to let you know there is hope. Hope that we may win the wedding of Petra Davos and Greg Breville—no guarantee but fingers and toes crossed. Love ya. Poppy xx

Done. A niggle of doubt touched her and she dismissed it. This was a real hope, a tangible hope, and Bella deserved that. There was no hope for herself and Nathan. No future.

A few minutes later they arrived, and as they headed to the restaurant she decided to stop playing foolish games, harbouring foolish hopes, and simply try to enjoy the evening.

Nathan looked round, instantly approved of the restaurant, intimate without being cloying, spacious but cosy, the music at the right levels and a general buzz that gave the idea of satisfied customers. Emphasised by the tantalising scents that lingered on the air.

Yet he suspected this evening he would find any setting positive because it was a background to Poppy's beauty. Though there was more than beauty in her appearance today, there was also something dangerous, a simmer, an edge that added an extra vibrancy, a sense of the unexpected that both exhilarated and wrongfooted him.

They were seated in a corner, the table illuminated by a trio of candles, and as they looked down at the menu Poppy gave a small nod, looked across at him. 'I think this is the one,' she said. 'It feels right, feels like it is all coming together.' She eyed him directly. 'Which is always a good thing, don't you think?'

It took a moment for the double entendre to hit and when he looked at her, saw the small saucy smile playing on her lips, he knew she'd done it deliberately, knew she was playing with fire, that the dress, the appearance, was all for him. 'It's something I always aim for,' he agreed smoothly, meeting the challenge in her eyes full on.

She gave a small unwilling gurgle of laughter and shook her head, looked back down at the menu.

'So what are you going to have?' she asked.

He looked at her and knew that what he really wanted right now wasn't food, or drink, or jazz. He wanted Poppy, with an intensity that scared him, that he had to ward off. Because it would be wrong. Wouldn't it? And for the first time he wasn't sure. Would it be so wrong? To do what? Kiss her again, hold her…? And then what?

How would that be fair? To anyone.

He looked back down at the menu, on some level saw that the restaurant promised local organic ingredients, had an extensive vegan selection. 'You go vegan,' she suggested, 'and I am going to try the organic chicken. That way we get a good idea of both ranges for Petra and Greg and their guests.'

He agreed and minutes later they gave the order to the waiter.

Once he'd gone, Nathan cleared his throat. 'OK, so this feels…odd,' he said. 'I guess it's because we're all dressed up, having dinner in a fancy restaurant, plans after, and I know we're doing this as research but it feels like…a date.' He shrugged. 'Not that I really remember what a date is like, but…it's like this, right?'

'It's been a while for me too.'

'It has?' He wanted to know and it seemed a fair enough question, seeing as he'd shared his own recent 'relationship'.

'About two years.'

'You haven't dated in two years?' Surprise laced his voice.

'Why so surprised?'

'I don't know. I thought, assumed…well, let's say I assumed someone as attractive as you would be pretty sought after. But even as I'm saying the words I can see that just because people are asking you on dates doesn't mean you have to say yes.'

'Actually, there haven't been a horde of men hammering on my door and even if there had been I haven't been interested. After the break-up with Steve, I have been on a dating sabbatical.' She looked him directly in the eye. 'Maybe that's why I can't really regret our kiss. It made me feel alive and it made me feel attractive.' She smiled up at the waiter as he brought their glasses of wine and starters.

He couldn't help it, the small snort of disbelief. 'But you're beautiful. You must know that you're attractive.'

'Not really. Not inside. Not after Steve.'

'Why. What did he do?' His hands had clenched into fists. 'If you like I'll go and find him and he can come here and apologise and tell you exactly how attractive you are.'

Now she smiled, let out a little laugh. 'It's OK. It's a tempting thought but I don't think that would be a good publicity move somehow.'

'Well, the offer stands. But on a serious note—tell me what happened. What went wrong?'

She hesitated for a minute, speared a wild mushroom with her fork and gave a rueful smile. 'Pretty much everything went wrong. But really it was my own fault. I was a fool. In brief, five years ago, my dad married wife number five, Natalia. About a month after the wedding Natalia asked me round for dinner, said she wanted to reunite the family. So Michael was there too and there were other people there as well, and one of those people was Steve. He was the son of a friend of Dad's and he was very attentive. Which also made me feel great. I felt like I had been invited into the fold. I felt...'

'You felt seen,' he said, knowing now, understanding now how important, how defining that must have been for her.

'That's it. Exactly. And I lost my head. It was all like a dream. After that dinner there was another and Steve was there again. Natalia told me he'd asked to be invited. I couldn't believe it, couldn't believe that maybe finally things were changing. Then Steve asked me out and Dad liked him, so sometimes Dad and Natalia would ask just me and Steve to dinner, or the races.'

'And Michael too?'

'No.' Now her voice held sadness. 'Part of it was because Michael was more cautious, less forgiving, more sceptical than me. Part of it was that they invited him less and blamed him for it.'

'How did he react?'

'He tried to warn me, told me Steve wasn't that good a guy, that I should be careful. But I didn't listen to him. Steve told me that Michael was jealous because Dad liked Steve. I believed him. I believed everything Steve said.' Her voice was bitter.

'You can't blame yourself for that.' But he could blame Steve, a mounting anger rising.

'Actually, yes, I can. I was a fool, a naïve idiot who saw what she wanted to see. And so the romance continued, encouraged by my dad, who really thought Steve was the bee's knees. Then Steve proposed. At a party in front of my dad, a public proposal, complete with a plane flying across the sky saying "Poppy, will you marry me?". Champagne and violins straight out of the fairy-tale playbook.'

'You could hardly have said no.'

'No. I couldn't have,' she agreed.

Nathan frowned. 'But fairy tale or not, that's not your sort of proposal.' Poppy gave him a swift surprised glance and he himself wondered how he could be so sure of that.

'You're right. I have always believed a proposal should be just the two of you and more… personal. In fact, I think that's when my doubts first started, when those rose-coloured spectacles started to demist a little. I mean, that was the sort of proposal my dad makes. Time and again. But I told myself I was being silly. Everything was great—why sabotage it? Dad was ecstatic, Natalia started to plan this big fancy wedding and I… I decided to let them get on with it and I made myself invisible. Dad gave us a house to live in, put Steve on the board of various companies.'

He got it. She must have felt invisible again and decided the best thing to do was remain unseen.

She waited whilst the waiters put their main courses in front of them.

'What happened?'

'Steve changed. Became less attentive, more secretive. I had the feeling something was off, that he was talking to other women, flirting, once I was sure I saw him getting a number. He dismissed my fears, of course, and I told myself I was being paranoid. That all men weren't my father and I mustn't, as he said, spoil our relationship with paranoia. Trust was everything.'

The bitterness in her voice was clear and anger touched him on her behalf. That any man could look at another woman when he had Poppy seemed impossible to him.

'It turned out trust was *nothing* to Steve. I can't believe it took me so long to figure out. I tried to believe him when he was late home, when he had meetings, but in the end I had to face the truth. He was cheating on me, big time. Worst of all was when I finally made him admit it he didn't understand what I was upset about. He said he thought I'd known what I was getting, that he was a man like my father and he wouldn't apologise for it. That we could still be happy, of course we could. That it was me he loved, the others weren't relevant.' Her voice broke on that and he saw the shudder of revulsion shake her body and the slow burn of anger that had grown throughout the whole sorry tale exploded.

'OK. That guy is a total loser and I am going to find him and kick him from here to tomorrow.'

'He's not worth it.' She shook her head. 'In the end I could see he was worth nothing. But then it all got even messier. I turfed him out, but my dad took his side, said Steve was like the son he always wanted That I should stand by him. That the house was Steve's.'

He could hear the bleakness in her voice, saw the shadow of memories cross her face and he felt her pain, could truly empathise with the deep sear of betrayal she must have felt then, knew it was a wound that she would still carry with her.

'I was such a fool, a gullible, naïve fool. And it's been hard to forget that. Hard to be interested in dating anyone. I tried once. Someone called Mark. He was a really nice man, I think. He seemed gentle, kind. But… I spent the whole time second-guessing myself. Was I right? Was he genuine? Was he lying? I found myself trying to catch him out, analysing everything he said, everything I said. In the end I figured it wasn't fair on him. He deserved someone better than me, someone who wasn't always looking for flaws, so I ended it. And truly since then I can't see the point. I've come to the same conclusions as you, but for different reasons. I'm not interested in a serious relationship either. I like my independence. I won't risk trusting anyone, including myself. I can't trust my own judgement.'

He shook his head. 'Maybe your judgement

was off with Steve but that's understandable. It wasn't about Steve, it was about being taken back into the family, your dad's approval. The happy ever after. You wanted it to be real. And I get that. Get how hard you tried to hold onto the dream, even when you knew it was wisping into illusion. How you rewrote the excuses and the lies into truths.'

'That is exactly how it was. How do you know?'

'Because that's how I felt about my dad. All those years I wanted him to be innocent. I wanted that belief to be real. And when I finally had to face I was wrong I felt like a fool.'

'But you weren't. You were a boy who wanted his dad to be different.'

'And you were a woman who wanted the same. If we were both fools then it was an understandable mistake. And you have to let that go. You can't let a slime ball like Steve wreck your self-confidence. Can't let your dad's or your mum's shortcomings affect your self-belief. You need to see yourself for who you are. See what you have achieved. Anyone else, after all you went through, would have given up and wallowed in despair. Turned to alcohol.'

As his mother had. 'You got on with life. You've started a new career, a new job that actually embraces love and marriage, despite your own experiences, and that takes courage and flair. And those are qualities you've always had in abundance. And now when the chips are down you're fighting. That takes guts. And…'

'There's more?' she asked.

'Yes, there is. You do have talent. You are a fashion princess. I get now why your self-belief has been shot. Anyone's would be. But somehow you need to find it again. Work on these sketches and designs and take them forward. I'm not saying ditch the wedding job. Add to it. Become a wedding company that also offers wedding-dress design. Specialise in that. Offer to design Petra's dress.' He beamed at her. 'See, that's a brilliant idea.'

Something sparked in her eyes, interest, self-belief, enthusiasm. And a sudden sensation of joy slipped through him. 'Hell, you could join forces with Petra, set up a design-agency-cum-model-agency-stroke-wedding-planning all under one name. There are so many possibilities. One day you could buy your parents out.'

That made her laugh out loud and he grinned. 'Unlikely scenario, but I'm liking it.'

'But you can't let them pull you down. They have shown their true colours and you, you, Poppy, you're way better than them.'

She pushed her plate away, reached out and covered his hand in hers. 'Thank you. Thank you for believing in me. It feels really, really good. Like I'm on top of the world.'

Her words filled him with a sudden sense of warmth, a pleasure that he'd done that for her, made her feel good about herself again. But before he could answer her phone rang out, the ringtone the 'Wedding March'. 'Sorry. I need to take this.' Her smile widened. 'It's Bella.'

'Go ahead. Take it.' He pushed his chair back and took his own phone out to give her some privacy.

She put the phone to her ear. 'Bella? Did you get my message? How is it all going?'

Then there was a silence, and he glanced up to see worry cross her face. With a small apologetic sign, she said, 'I'll be back soon,' then rose and headed towards the door.

CHAPTER FOURTEEN

POPPY PUSHED THE door of the restaurant open and headed back to the table, her brain processing the conversation with her friend and wondering what she should do.

'Poppy? Is everything OK?'

'Yes. No. Well, sort of.' She sat down and looked across at Nathan.

'I've ordered coffee,' he said. 'And a mini chocolate mousse. I thought chocolate may help.'

The act of thoughtfulness warmed her, brought a quick smile to her face. 'Thank you. Chocolate always helps.'

She sat down, smiled up at the waiter who brought over the coffee and mousses, focused on eating, on the rich, dark taste of the chocolate, the warm strength of the coffee. It was only when she'd finished that he spoke.

'Do you want to talk about it?'

To her own surprise she did and she wasn't sure how she felt about that. Because she didn't know whether she should share the conversation or not. Bella had told her she trusted her, to use her discretion.

'Do what you think is best, Poppy. I trust you. To do whatever is best for the proposal. For the business. I am sorry that I can't help more.'

Of course she'd told Bella not to apologise; her friend had nothing to be sorry for. But now she had to work out the best thing to do. How much to confide in Nathan.

'Bella won't be able to be part of organising the wedding. Or at least not initially. And I'm good with that. I'm confident I can do it myself. If need be I can hire a temporary assistant. But I'm worried how Petra will react. After all, Bella is the senior partner.'

Nathan drummed his fingers on the tabletop in thought. 'They will ask why Bella can't be involved.'

'I know.'

'Can you tell me the answer?'

'I can. I don't know if I should. Because once I tell you, you may feel obliged to tell Petra and Greg and I'm not sure yet if I think that is necessary or a good idea.'

'I won't tell without your permission.' His voice was even, deep with sincerity. 'You have my word.'

His word. Nathan's word. Was she a fool to

believe him? After all, Steve had given her his word and broken it more times than she cared to count. Her father, too, was notorious for breaking any promise he undertook, from wedding vows to a simple 'I promise to come and see you next weekend.'

'It's up to you, Poppy, but if telling me will help then you can tell me in confidence. If you trust me.'

And as she looked across the table, saw his face in the flicker of candlelight, saw the jut of his jaw, the truth in his eyes, she knew on a gut level that she could. But her instincts had failed her before and this wasn't only about her. Because if she got this wrong, if she trusted Nathan and the result was losing this proposal, she'd never forgive herself.

'Can I think on it? Just until we get to the jazz club. We still need to check that out and… I need to go back to London tomorrow, if I can change my flight.' She wanted to see Bella. Make sure her friend was OK. She felt suddenly bereft as she said the words; the decision was correct but it meant one day less with Nathan.

And she thought she saw her own sadness mirrored in his grey eyes and then, 'I understand.' He rose to his feet and reached out a hand. 'Truly I do. This proposal makes all the difference and the pressure has upped a notch. You need to get it straight in your head. Take your time. And whilst you do let's go listen to some jazz.'

She put her hand in his and let him pull her to her feet, and as she did she felt the now familiar frisson of awareness, but this time there was something else too, a sense of trust and a hint of regret that the mood of the evening had changed.

An hour later they entered the jazz club, situated in a small, unassuming alleyway, and as the attendant swung the lightly coloured door open, despite everything, Poppy felt an uplift to her spirits as the strains of music wafted out onto the night air.

They entered and she focused on her first impressions, loved the instant feeling of intimacy and of almost travelling back in time. The walls were hung with black and white photos of previous performers and she knew she could happily spend an hour studying them. Small square wooden tables dotted the floor and there was a busy bar on one side of the room. But best of all was the music, the notes of the trombone quivering on the air.

She followed Nathan to a spare table and sat down, closed her eyes and let the music engulf her.

'I'll get us a drink,' he said. 'What would you like?'

'Surprise me,' she said.

He returned to the table a few minutes later and handed her a glass. 'It's a sidecar,' he said. 'Apparently it's the perfect cocktail to have in a jazz club. Cointreau, cognac, lemon juice and sugar syrup.'

'Thank you.' She took a sip and turned to him. 'Can I ask you something?'

'Of course.'

'You said I could trust you not to tell Petra and Greg. Why are you willing to promise that? What if you feel they need to know?'

'The answer to that is simple. I trust you. I trust your professional integrity. If you feel this information, whatever it is, would impact adversely on their wedding then you would tell them. You wouldn't risk their wedding. Because that would be both morally wrong and professionally stupid. So you wouldn't do it. I know that.'

'OK.' That made sense and she appreciated his explanation, because it made it easier for her to rationalise the blind instinct that told her it was safe to confide in him, to trust his word. 'So this is the situation. Bella is a recovering alcoholic. It's not common knowledge at all, she only told me because she felt it was fair before we went into partnership. We didn't discuss it again after that. Until the whole fiasco with Della Mac's wedding. Bella started to unravel and in the end she admitted she wasn't coping, had started drinking again. So we booked her into a clinic; I was advised that the best thing would be for her to focus on recovery and not have contact with the outside world for the first couple of weeks at least, though she would have limited access to her phone if she wished.'

'So Bella doesn't know about the proposal for Petra and Greg?'

'She didn't till today. I messaged her earlier. I wanted to give her some hope, let her know things may be looking up.'

'So that's why she called you?'

'Yes.' Poppy took a deep breath. 'She told me things aren't going that great. She had a relapse. She actually discharged herself from the clinic and went on a bit of a bender. But she is back in now and she says she is doing OK. But she says her therapist says, and she agrees, that she can't deal with all the pressure of a high-profile wedding right now.'

Poppy closed her eyes. 'Maybe I shouldn't have done this, should never have tried to get this off the ground.' Should never have ambushed Nathan in his office. All else aside, Poppy knew she couldn't regret that, couldn't regret the last few days. 'Bella says she will leave it to me, she'll understand if I don't want to go ahead by myself.'

'And do you?'

'Of course I do. I want to save Star Weddings. And I believe I can pull this off for Petra and Greg, even without Bella. Or at least I think I can. But what if I'm wrong? Or what if Petra and Greg disagree? And surely they have the right to make that decision themselves. But is it fair to tell them the truth? About Bella? How can I trust them to keep it confidential? If news like that leaks out, it will be no good for future business. Plus if I tell them and they decide to pull the plug, then Star Weddings goes down the plughole.'

'Whoa. Slow down. I get these are tough decisions but... I think you've answered your own question. You believe you can do this on your own. Why would Petra and Greg doubt you?'

'Because...because I'm the junior partner.'

'Doesn't matter. You have the experience. You're the one who worked on the proposal and you have my backing. One hundred per cent. And you have no choice. You either give up or you keep going.'

The words made sense and the fact he would back her made her lips curve upwards. 'Thank you for the validation. For being here, for being the voice of reason, for helping. But how do I explain it to them?'

'What did Bella suggest?'

'She said she'd leave it to me. And…' Poppy hesitated. 'I didn't want to push her. She sounded fragile enough as it was. I shouldn't—' She broke off.

'What shouldn't you have done?'

'I shouldn't have told her about the proposal. I wish she'd told me about the relapse; she said she felt too ashamed. I wish I'd realised how much she was struggling sooner. Back when we were organising Della Mac's wedding. I should have thought, should have been more supportive. I should have been there for her. And now, now what if I mess up? I have to make this work. For Bella. Or she'll come out of rehab and I'll have lost her Star Weddings.'

'Don't.' He reached out, covered her hand in his. 'You cannot blame or second-guess yourself. Or fix this for Bella. Alcoholism isn't like that—it's not as simple. However much you care about the other person, you can't beat yourself up about what you should and shouldn't have done. I know that, Poppy. I've seen it with my mum.'

She looked at him, saw the pain in his face, knew he was only willing to talk about this to help her. 'You never really talked about your mum. About her drinking.'

'You didn't need to know. It felt disloyal to my mother to discuss her, plus it became second nature to keep it hidden. From teachers, social workers, everyone really. It became part of my life, but I didn't need to talk about it, didn't want pity or for it to define me in your eyes.'

'I'm sorry. You were still a child. You shouldn't have had to go through that.' She hoped he could hear the emotion in her voice, not pity, but a simple compassion, an acknowledgement that it wasn't fair.

'Perhaps. But I didn't mind. At first I was holding the fort until my dad came back, proved innocent. And then, then I was determined to right the wrong he'd done. I'd make it up to my mum. Give her back what she'd lost.'

'Fix things.'

'That's the mistake I made. I thought I could fix things. Fix her.' He sounded sad. 'I truly believed that if I could give her back all she'd lost, the house, the money, the lifestyle, she'd stop drinking. It seemed so clear-cut to me. But it didn't work.'

He cradled his glass in his hand, stared at the stage where the artist was still playing a haunting tune that filled the club with motes of might-have-beens. 'She tried, you know, she really tried. But in the end the alcohol won. She said she needed it, to give her confidence, to keep the demons away, for a bit of Dutch courage, to relax her.'

He shrugged. 'I have tried to persuade her to go to a clinic, but she doesn't want to. And who am I to judge? Over the past years she has drunk less, had times when she hasn't drunk at all, but it is still there. And I spent years second-guessing. Wondering if I should have told the social workers, should have done things differently, been different, been there, worked more, worked less…but in the end I've realised I can't think like that. I can try and help but I can't make choices for her. Just like you can't for Bella. You can be supportive, you can help, but in the end the choices are Bella's. But, for what it's worth, it sounds to me as though she is making the right ones. She is trying.'

Poppy took a deep breath. 'Thank you. Truly. Sharing that has truly helped me. So I'll give it my best shot. To convince Petra and Greg I can go it alone and I think… I think I'll tell them the truth about Bella. Because I think what Bella is doing, trying to fight addiction, is something that should be celebrated, something she should be proud of, not something that is hidden. But…only if Petra and Greg keep it to themselves. I also don't want Bella's problems splashed across the papers.'

'I trust Greg and Petra, but…' He hesitated. 'In all truth there is every chance that some enterprising reporter will find out the truth anyway. And Bella will have to deal with that. That's what my mum can't do—deal with life without alcohol to prop her up. But it sounds as though that's what Bella is trying to figure out and I truly hope she does it.'

'So do I. She said today that she is trying to face up to things, things she regrets or wishes she'd done differently. Things from the past.' She frowned. 'She asked me to call Michael.'

He paused, his drink halfway to his lips. 'Your brother Michael?'

'Yes. I don't know why. I didn't even know they knew each other. But she asked me to call him to ask him to call her tomorrow.'

'Are you going to?'

'Yes. I am.' Even though she hadn't spoken to Michael for months, even though she didn't understand how he and Bella knew each other. 'She said facing the past will give her closure, help her move on.'

'Then you need to call him.'

'I'll do that now. And I'll get us another drink on the way back.'

'Sounds good.'

CHAPTER FIFTEEN

NATHAN TRIED TO focus on the stage, on the music, on the ambiance as he waited for Poppy to return, but somehow all of it seemed to fade as he sat, fingers drumming on the table, hoping she was all right.

Hoping he'd made a difference—helped her get some perspective on Bella's plight. Hoped now that the conversation with Michael was going well, that her brother didn't continue to hold Poppy responsible for their father's shortcomings. Hoped— His thoughts broke off as he saw her walking back to the table and his heart gave a sudden lurch. She was so goddam beautiful.

She placed the drinks on the table and sat down, her expression pensive but not upset, as far as he could discern.

'How did it go?'

'Actually. It was fine. I mean, I am none the wiser about how he knows Bella, but he agreed to call her and we've agreed to meet up when I get back to London. I should have rung him years ago—instead of hiding, feeling guilty, avoiding him. My dad betrayed both of us, and God knows I wish I'd listened to Michael about Steve. But I didn't and it's time for us to move on.' She picked up her drink. 'Hell, maybe Michael and I will go and talk to my dad, say our piece, get some closure.' She paused, shrugged. 'And maybe you should too.'

'Excuse me?'

'Or maybe your mum should. Track down your dad. Say her piece. Face the past. And then move on from it.'

'I told you. It's a bad idea.'

The idea of seeing his father made him want to squirm, shift on the wooden seat in discomfort. Get up and pace around. Thump the table, punch the wall.

'Maybe if your mum met him, saw the man he is today, it may give her closure. Be it anger, forgiveness, apologies, a row… But she would stop remembering the past and see what he has become. Maybe it would give your mum some peace. Allow her to really move on, with a new life.'

Could Poppy be right? Could it be that seeing the man who had destroyed her life would somehow enable his Mum to move on?

She sipped her drink, unconsciously swaying slightly to the music. 'I mean, in some ways isn't that what we're doing? This time we've spent together—it's been important, hasn't it? We've talked and connected and made our peace. And tomorrow we'll move on.'

Her words caught him, like a short, sharp thud to his solar plexus. Soon, tomorrow, Poppy would be out of his life for good, for ever. There would no longer be an annual text, no longer a need to recall her birthday, no reason to recall her at all. Except as someone from his past, a friendship closed down, closed off, permanently shut down. He'd never find out how her meeting with Michael went, see any more of her fashion sketches, go cycling with her...

The idea caused a sudden sense of urgency, a need to look at her, imprint her on his mind. And as he looked, his gaze lingered on her face, the classic slant of her cheekbones, the wide green eyes, flecked with emerald specks of differing emotions. Took in the rich hue of her hair, tresses he wanted to entangle his fingers in.

And then the dress, the vibrant red material that clung to her figure, the bare shoulders that he wanted to touch with a desire that made him dizzy, and then up to her lips, lips he could remember the taste, the texture, the glorious feel of. Lips that curved up into a smile that lit her face, the smooth brow that creased in thought, as it did now.

'Have I got something on my nose?'

'Nope. I…'

'Then why were you looking at me like that?'

'Because you're beautiful. The most beautiful woman in this room. It seems important that you should know that.'

'Thank you. Really. I…' Her cheeks flushed and she gave a half-embarrassed laugh. 'Are you just trying to change the subject?'

'No. I'm not. But you're right. We haven't got much time left and I… I don't know, it seemed important to tell you.' He shook his head. 'Sorry. Now I feel a bit foolish.'

'Don't. Actually…you saying that makes me feel a bit guilty.'

'Why?'

'Because I put this dress on, did my best with my make-up, in order to make you see what you are missing.'

'For real?'

'Yes. It sounds silly but after our kiss, when I could see the guilt on your face, I think it messed with my head a bit. Because since Steve I hadn't kissed *anybody*—not even Mark and I dated him for months. Because I felt unattractive, a bit grubby.'

He couldn't hold back the snort. 'Steve was a slimeball.' He leant forward across the dimly lit table, moved the candle out of the way so he could take her hands, grasped them firmly, registered the soft coolness of her skin, the slender fingers.

'Listen to me, Poppy. It's nothing to do with the dress, even though you look stunning in it, or the make-up. To me you'd be the most beautiful woman in here if you were dressed in a bin bag. And that's the truth.' He leant back and smiled at her. 'Now, I have an idea. Let's put the past behind us. Right now. And let's dance.'

She looked at him wide-eyed. 'You sure that's a good idea?'

'I think it's the best idea I've had in a long time.'

There were so many reasons not to dance but Poppy didn't care. Didn't care there was no dance floor, only a few couples stood swaying in between the tiny square wooden tables, didn't even care they might draw attention. In truth the people in here were interested in the music, in each other, and in the dimly lit room no one would notice them.

But it wasn't about practicalities—it was a bad idea because she wasn't sure what would happen if they danced together, up close, intimate.

And yet she rose to her feet, knew it wasn't possible to refuse—she felt alive, vibrant, and for the first time in so long she felt attractive, beautiful, desirable as an individual. Nathan had eyes for no other woman in here, wasn't scanning the area for further conquests. His grey eyes were unwavering and focused on her, dark with desire for Poppy.

'Then let's do it.'

She stood and put her hand in his, revelled in the strength of his fingers, and then he'd pulled her into his arms and she was lost. There wasn't room for anything complicated, instead he pulled her body against his and the fit was perfect, and as the notes from the sax and the trombone quivered on the air and the singer's rich voice delivered the poignant lyrics of love, they moved together as if they had been born for this.

The strength of his chest, the muscular beauty of him, made her boneless, fluid. As she moved to the beat of the music it felt as though the club faded away and it were just them, locked in a timeless dance. She could feel the beat of his heart, and then as the sax went into a glorious solo she looked up at him and she knew what would happen next, welcomed it as he kissed her, and this time the sensations were both new and familiar, the taste of Cointreau, the dizzying, heady, soaring elation as the music reached the crescendo and her whole being was subsumed in the moment, in the heat of desire.

Until the music stopped, and as the last lingering note died away they both stepped back and she put her hand out to steady herself. Looked up at him, relieved to see that this time there was no grimness, no regrets, simply a look of shell shock, as though the kiss had been as seismic for him as it had been for her.

'I...' Words were impossible to find. All she could do right now was feel, yearn, relive the kiss.

'It's OK.' He put a hand out, laid a finger on her lips. 'It's OK,' he repeated, and she nodded as they made their way back to the table.

Poppy blinked, and glanced round—no one was watching them, everyone had turned back to the band, who had now embarked on a much faster foot-tapping melody. They sat, let the music wash over them and then Poppy took a deep breath. Somehow the events of the past day coalesced into a knowledge of what to do next.

'Nathan?' His name was half question. 'I've got an idea.'

'Go ahead.'

'That kiss was…'

'Amazing, wonderful, glorious.' His words an affirmation that gave her the courage to continue.

'All of those things but it also wasn't enough. I want… I want more. I want you.' She hurried on before he could say anything. 'I know everything you said yesterday, I know you think this is wrong. But it doesn't have to be. Neither of us wants a relationship, and I fully understand why you want me out of your life.' The words were a torrent now and he reached out, oh, so gently, and put a finger to her lips.

'I want you too. So much that right now it is taking every bit of my willpower to sit here, not touching you, not kissing you.'

The world went still, the music, the people became a faded low-level noise, though she knew it was a melody she would never forget.

'Good. That's good,' she said, the words half groan as she wrapped her hands round her glass to keep them from reaching out to him. 'So this is what I think we should do. I think we have this night, this one night left, and I think we should spend it together. It's one night.' Alexis wouldn't grudge them that. 'Our deal still stands. I will exit your life. That's best for us both—we're agreed on that. But we won't look back and wonder, there won't be any what-ifs. Plus…' she tried a smile '…I'm not sure how long it will be before my libido resurfaces so I'd really like to take this opportunity whilst I can.'

She came to a halt, watched his expression. Any minute now her heart was going to pop out of her chest. Its pounding was telling her how insane the idea was. She realised she'd opened herself up to more rejection. The flicker of doubt was erased by his expression, the sheer, unmistakable passion in his grey eyes. She saw him clench his hands around the table edge, could see desire war with the need to be sure.

Then. 'You sure?'

She couldn't help her smile, the knowledge that here and now they were in synch, and as he studied her expression in turn, she willed him to see that she was. Sure that, whatever the future held, right now this was what she wanted, and she knew the cost of not doing it. The regrets would far outweigh any regrets that she already had.

And now he smiled. 'Silly question. All we can be sure of is that this is what we both want in the here and now and… I don't want us to talk ourselves out of it. I want you, Poppy Winchester. I want you right now.'

'And I want you, Nathan Larrimore. So bad that I may literally combust on the spot.'

'Then what are we waiting for? Let's go.'

He rose to his feet and she did the same, gave a half-laugh. 'Lucky I can walk fast in these,' she said, indicating her shoes.

'No need to rush,' he said. 'Anticipation can be fun.'

She gulped. 'It can?'

'Yup. So whilst we walk back I can tell you exactly what I have planned.'

Oh, God. She really might go up in flames and as his eyes lingered on her, her body craved his touch, her skin tingled, her nerves strummed, her muscles clenched.

She grabbed his hand. 'And by the time I've told you my plans I think you'll be walking pretty damn fast.'

In the end they entered the hotel at a half run, breathless with laughter and desire, raced to the lift and when it took too long to arrive, by tacit consent they took the stairs.

'Which room?'

'Mine's closest.'

'Decision made.'

Nathan swiped his key card, saw that his fingers were trembling, his whole being consumed with his need for the woman next to him. He didn't know how this had happened, didn't care, knew that this felt right, everything she'd said had made sense, a wonderful sense that allowed them to act on this need for each other, this physical need that could now be assuaged—the night stretching ahead with a glorious abandon.

Now they were inside and they turned to each other, all foolish ambition to take things slow seen now as foolish bravado. Because all that mattered was this, greedy fingers tearing at clothing, as they moved in tandem towards the bed. One impatient move swept away the clothes left there earlier, the sheets of paper where he'd been jotting formulae swept in a flutter to the floor as he tumbled her back onto the soft silkiness of the duvet. And then there was only this…only Poppy.

Nathan opened his eyes filled with an enormous sense of well-being, remaining as still as possible in order not to wake Poppy, who was still asleep, her head resting on his chest, her hair a welcome tickle, one arm slung around him.

The previous hours had been so full of joy and laughter and sheer overwhelming relief. And now…as he stared up at the bright white of the ceiling, as sleep receded, a cold, harsh fact occurred to him. At no point, not one in the previous evening, had Alexis crossed his mind. It had all been about Poppy. From the moment they'd set out for the restaurant, he'd been consumed by her.

The realisation was a punch to his gut, as now different emotions started to surge upwards.

Poppy's voice: *'Thank you for being here, for being the voice of reason, for helping.'*

Alexis's words in her diary.

You were never here, Nathan. Never here for me. I never felt you listened. There was always an idea, always a project, all those late nights, all those times away, all the putting off. No children...

When Poppy had suggested last night he'd agreed without thought, no sense of betrayal. His only concern had been if Poppy was sure it was the right decision.

He'd slept with the woman who Alexis had believed he'd always wanted.

'I saw the two of you together.'

'Would you have ignored her like you did me?'

He tried to remain still but Poppy stirred, opened her eyes and smiled at him and he knew, knew he couldn't tell her his thoughts. Wouldn't hurt her like that. This wasn't her fault. At all. And the previous night had been magical and wonderful. The guilt, the discomfort he was feeling was his and his alone to deal with.

And so he smiled; even now her beauty touched him, the sleep-crumpled face, the dishevelled red hair. The green eyes studying him with way too much acumen as her forehead creased into a frown.

'Morning.'

'Morning.' He cleared his throat, tried again. 'Morning. How are you feeling?' What sort of question was that? 'I'm feeling hungry—so what do you say we head down and have a massive breakfast? Yum-yum.' He winced, could hardly blame her frown for deepening as she shifted away from him, sat up, pulling the duvet up with her.

'Nathan, what's wrong?'

'Absolutely nothing.' The hearty approach. 'Or at least nothing a good breakfast won't solve.'

Before she could answer her phone rang out, the ringtone the sound of the 'Wedding March'. 'I need to get that. It's Bella.'

She glanced at him again and he could see worry and wariness cross her eyes, before she reached down and snagged her dress. 'It's OK.' He slid out of bed and scrambled into his jeans, went to the bathroom and came back with one of the fluffy bathrobes.

'Thanks.' She climbed out of bed and picked up her phone. 'Bella.'

As she spoke Nathan took the opportunity to pull a T-shirt over his head, saw her glance at him. 'Thank you, Bella. For letting me know. I'll come and see you as soon as I'm back.'

She put the phone back on the desk and turned to Nathan. 'She was calling to reassure me; I think she knew I felt bad yesterday. She says knowing there is hope for Star Weddings makes her happy but if it all goes wrong it won't be on me. At all. She will survive. So no pressure. And she said Michael is going round to see her today, so turns out there is no need for me to rush back as the clinic only allows one visit a day.' She shrugged. 'So I am still not sure what is going on there, but this does give us one more day and night.'

'That's good.' Though he knew exactly how unenthusiastic he sounded as panic swirled inside him. 'Great news.'

'What's wrong? I thought you'd be pleased.' She stepped forward, one hand held out, and how he wanted to step forward, take that hand, pick her up, twirl her round and take her straight back to the crumpled bed. Instead he took a step back, could feel panic etch itself on his face, saw confusion morph to a profound hurt on hers.

She dropped her hand, took a step backwards of her own. 'You're not pleased,' she said, and her voice tightened. 'I… I don't get it.' She took a deep breath and he could see her try to marshal her thoughts. 'It's only twenty-four hours more. I wasn't expecting, I wasn't wanting anything more than that. But I'm guessing you were always after a one-night stand, nothing more.' She looked at him and her voice cracked slightly. 'Is that what your rules are?'

'No. There aren't any rules.'

The expression on her face—the hurt gone now, replaced by an icy hardness, an almost cruel twist to her lips. 'Really? Was last night simply another physical release for you and now you're good for another few years?' She shook her head. 'I cannot believe I was such a fool again. To think I may be worth an extra night. Tell me. Last night if I'd suggested we have two days together, three days, would you still have agreed?'

'I… I don't know. Last night, all I could think about was you. Nothing else. No one else. Only you.'

'And what am I supposed to feel? Flattered?'

'No.' He closed his eyes, wanted somehow to try to grasp this conversation before everything unravelled. 'Last night was…wonderful, amazing, magical… I can't find words for it.

Joyful…it was way more than physical release and it was more than physical. There was a connection.' One that had transcended physical. He shook his head, ran a hand through his hair. 'If it was just physical release, we'd be back in that bed now.'

'So what are you saying?'

'I'm saying we have to stop now, that any more is too…much, too dangerous. It would feel wrong.'

'Does last night feel wrong?'

'No…yes. I don't know.' He drew in a breath. 'You have done nothing wrong.'

'But you believe you have. Is it Alexis?'

The name sliced through the air, conjured up images of his wife, the woman he'd loved and let down, the woman he'd sidelined.

'Because I don't get it. I don't believe Alexis would grudge you two nights of joy, a connection with someone else. A bubble of time—that isn't a betrayal of what you had.'

'But it is.'

'Why?' She looked at him, her green eyes so vivid, so piercing, he almost winced. 'It's because it's me, isn't it?' She stepped forward, her eyes wide now, pleading almost. 'But that doesn't matter. I know I am linked to your past, I know I can't be part of your future, but why can't this be all right? What we have now? Why do you feel you've done something wrong? I was never part of your marriage, barely part of your life once you met Alexis. I doubt she even gave me a thought. So why are you feeling like this?'

CHAPTER SIXTEEN

POPPY STARED AT NATHAN, tried to quell, push down, eliminate the searing hurt. What did it matter? One night or two? Yet the sting, the stab of rejection felt like the gape of a wound. She clenched her hands into fists, willed herself to behave with at least a semblance of dignity.

Nathan's reaction was hardly a surprise—he still loved Alexis, and for him last night had been a betrayal of that love. Simple. For Poppy it had been an incredible journey of sheer sensory joy, the gratification, the need for each other, the softness of laughter, the feel of his hands on her body, the touch of him, the taste of him... The glory of the hours had filled her with happiness and exhilaration that had stayed with her when she opened her eyes.

But for Nathan the morning had brought bleakness and guilt, his mind and heart filled with thoughts of Alexis.

So why was she even questioning him—was

she some sort of masochist? Did she want him to actually spell it out for her? What *did* it matter? One night or two?

It wasn't as though she'd suggested they try out a real relationship, try to build on their connection, try to make a go of it. Not as if they'd fallen in love. The idea was ludicrous... Only right now as she looked at him, at this man who she'd shared so much with in the past days, the man she'd confided in and who had confided in her, the man who believed, truly believed in her talent, the man who had brought her libido back to life, the man who had had eyes only for her...realisation dawned, bleak and desolate— he was also the man she'd fallen in love with.

No, no, no! No way!

Because he might only have had eyes for her last night, but his heart belonged to someone else, someone Poppy could never compete with, never be better than. As it had been with Sylvia, with her mother's other family. With all of Steve's women.

So she would wrench this love out, refuse it space. And so she would demand the answer to her question. Have it spelled out for her, welcome the pain as it would kill love before it could take hold.

'Why, Nathan? Why are you feeling so guilty?

Why are you making something that I believed to be beautiful into something tawdry?'

'It wasn't tawdry.' The words pulled from him. 'But it was a betrayal of Alexis. Because she did give you a thought, because you were part of our marriage. I just didn't know it.'

'I don't understand.'

'After she died, I found a diary. In it she said she believed, had believed throughout our marriage, that I had feelings for you. That if you hadn't left I would never have pursued a relationship with her, never married her.'

'But that's not true.'

'That's what I thought. I put it down to a sick woman's fancy, believed the drugs had caused a temporary delusion. But now…now I don't know. These past days, last night. Until now I have always known I could look Alexis in the eye and tell her her fear was unfounded. Now… I don't know what I would tell her, but I do know to continue this, even for one more night, is wrong.'

Poppy looked at him as the words took meaning. She'd done it again, caused a marriage to flounder, a love to be betrayed. With her mother it had been done in innocence, with no malice, she'd been a catalyst. But now, she couldn't plead innocence. She'd known Nathan was in love with his wife, but she'd forged on.

Flirted, bantered and kissed him, kissed him again. And she hadn't done what she'd known she should. She hadn't made herself invisible, hadn't disappeared herself. On and on she'd gone, last night she'd deliberately dressed to entice, to lure, dressed to kill. Until she'd brought this about. This pain on his face.

OK. Sure, she hadn't known about Alexis's diary but that meant nothing. She'd known how Nathan felt. So now she would do what she could do to make amends.

'Nathan, you have done nothing wrong. Once you and I were close friends. Nothing more. Alexis was threatened by that but she had no need to be. When I walked away you didn't follow. You had a new life, with the woman you loved, the woman you married. In that perfect wedding ceremony, where all you thought about was her happiness. Our friendship—it died a natural death.

'Then we were thrown together, we've both been hurt, we both knew from the past we could trust each other and we've both been celibate. That's all—our attraction happened because it felt safe, and because we both knew we were going our separate ways again. That's it. You have done nothing wrong, and I do truly believe that Alexis would agree. One night, physical relief, a connection forged on the very grounds of it being temporary, dissolvable. And now it's time to dissolve it permanently.'

Now she did move towards him.

'It's time to say goodbye.' To do what she should have done from the start. Disappear herself. 'And please believe this. You have done nothing wrong and I wish you all the luck in the world going forward. Because that's what we've always believed. The importance of moving forward.'

Now finally he broke his silence. 'Goodbye, Poppy. Thank you…for everything. And I hope all your dreams come true.'

How she wanted to move forward and kiss him one last time, but she wouldn't. She'd done enough and now all that was left to do was retreat, and hope he didn't hear the crack of her heart as she did so.

'Come in.' Nathan looked up from his desk as the door swung open. 'Greg, what can I do for you?'

He met his friend and partner's gaze, wished Greg would stop finding reasons to come in to talk to him. Saw the concern in the other man's eyes. Damn it, he didn't want concern. Loathed that Greg even knew there was anything wrong.

'Is there an administrative point you need to raise, or do you need to check a fact or ask a question that I know you already have the an-swer to?'

Greg grinned at him. 'Good to see your sense of sarcasm is still intact. Actually, I did have a question, but it's one I don't know the answer to.'

'Go ahead.'

'Poppy is coming round for dinner tonight to discuss the wedding plans—would you like to come too?'

A chance to see Poppy again, in person, rather than in his dreams both waking and sleeping. Because her image haunted him, wisps of memories, laughter, the glint of sun-shine on red hair, and then always the look of hurt. A hurt that he'd caused with his rejection of her. A rejection that tore and seared him with regret and frustration and misery. But one he could do nothing about—nothing but throw himself into work, his negotiations for the new business about to come to fruition, the publicity campaign started, the almost feverish work on the new car and any spare time spent on try-ing to crack the vegan formula that eluded him.

But through it all, at the periphery of his brain was Poppy. But it would have to cease, the image would have to fade eventually. It had when she'd walked away from their friend-ship. And it would now. But not if he yielded to temptation and saw her. More than that, he wouldn't go because it wouldn't be fair to Poppy. She'd succeeded in winning Petra and Greg's approval, told them the truth about Bella and the wedding plans were surging ahead. He wouldn't wrongfoot her with his presence and why would she want to see him? She was doing the right thing—she was moving on. And he was glad for her.

'Thank you, but no. I'm about to leave now— I'm meeting my mother for dinner tonight.'

Which at least had the virtue of truth, he thought as he sat opposite his mother in the popular, upmarket restaurant and tried not to imagine Poppy sitting with Petra and Greg, the way she would look, her beautiful face lit with enthusiasm as she made suggestions, the frown of concentration as she listened, really listened to what they had to say.

'Nathan?' His mum's voice broke into his thoughts.

'Sorry, Mum. I was miles away.'

'It's OK. Thinking of Poppy?'

Nathan choked on his sparkling water and attempted nonchalance. 'Why would I be thinking of Poppy?'

Katie Larrimore gave a sudden mischievous grin and sipped from her glass of wine. 'I can't imagine. Because she is beautiful, funny, talented, and you've just spent days with her.'

'As a favour to Greg and Petra,' Nathan said through gritted teeth. 'And how do you know all this anyway?'

'Because I dropped into your offices to see you when you were away and Greg and I had a lovely chat.'

Nathan eyed his mother, took in the newly done hair, registered that she was still on her barely touched first glass of wine and he was pretty sure she'd been stone-cold sober when she arrived as well. 'That's wonderful,' he said. 'But I don't want to talk about Poppy. But I would like to talk about you. Something has changed.'

His mum took a deep breath. 'I'm not getting too excited about it or anything but I... Well, I've met someone.' Nathan blinked. 'And before you say anything, I didn't meet him at a party when I was drunk, or when I'd even had a drink.'

'I wasn't going to say that,' Nathan protested. Though he knew why his mum thought he might have. The few relationships his mum had had since his dad had gone to prison had been alcohol-fuelled encounters, or brief liaisons that had focused round drink. 'So tell me.'

'I met him when he was walking his dog.

The dog, called Sandy, slipped his lead and ran away. I saw him and I managed to catch him. Ted came running up soon after and we got talking and we went to coffee so he could thank me and...then he invited me to an art gallery.' She smiled suddenly. 'He's an amateur painter and he's showing me how to paint. And I'm loving it.'

'Mum. I am so pleased for you.'

'So am I. And it's strange, Nathan. I don't feel the need to drink as much right now. But that's not what I want to talk about. I know you don't want to talk about Poppy and I know I have no right to interfere in your life, but please don't let the past hold you back from finding happiness. Because that's what I have done. All my sadness and bitterness and anger with your father, I couldn't work out how to move on from it. And I'm sorry. It stopped me from seeing what I did have. I had you.'

'You still do, Mum.' He took a deep breath. 'Do you think finding Dad, seeing him, would help?'

His mum stilled, her hand going out to her wine glass, but though she cradled the stem she didn't lift it. 'I don't know,' she said finally. 'Perhaps. Perhaps it would bring closure, an understanding that he was part of my life, our life, and perhaps an understanding of how he could have done what he did. Let me think on it.'

He nodded.

'But it's not your dad, is it? For you? It's Alexis. Don't let your grief, your emotions around Alexis keep you from happiness in the here and now. And, Nathan, don't take it all on yourself. All the responsibility. Life is complicated, love is complicated, the past is complicated, but I do know this. You deserve to be happy. And so does Poppy.' She smiled. 'Now, enough of that. What else would you like to talk about?'

'Art,' Nathan said promptly. 'Tell me more about what you are doing.' And as he spoke with his mum, felt a simple happiness that she didn't drink more than one glass of wine, as she spoke of her painting, of Ted, about the dog, Sandy, he felt a hope and a happiness for her. And he knew what he had to do next.

Poppy held her breath as she watched Petra's face as the blonde woman studied the sketchbook. Her expression unreadable, her blue eyes intent as she turned the pages, forward and then back. Finally she put the book down and turned to Poppy.

'It's perfect. And you designed this?'

'Yes. With you in mind and for the wedding

you have chosen.' Poppy forced herself to try to sound professional, but she couldn't keep the pride out of her voice. 'As you can see, you can wear the long version for the ceremony and the lunch afterwards. Then it can be converted into something shorter and sassy that you can easily ride the bumper cars on. You'll have different shoes, of course, and I can easily incorporate a change of hairstyle if you want as well. I've got it all figured out. But only if you like it.'

'I love it. It's unique, bespoke and part of my wedding package. And you'll make it.'

'Yes. I'll make it.' Poppy gestured towards the sketchbook. 'Providing, of course, you also agree to the price. I've given you a discount to say thank you for taking a chance on Star Weddings and for understanding about Bella.'

'The price is fine. I'll transfer you the deposit today.'

'Great.' Poppy rose to her feet, wished she didn't have the ridiculous urge to call Nathan, the desire so strong it hurt. She wanted to share this with him, show him the sketches, thank him for the support he'd given her and his belief in her. Wanted to know how he was doing, whether he was OK.

Of course he was OK—why wouldn't he be? She knew Nathan—he might be worried about how Poppy was doing, would be feeling bad or concerned for how he'd treated her. But the bottom line was he didn't want to be with her. Or rather he believed it was wrong to be with her, a betrayal of Alexis, the love of his life. The woman Poppy could never live up to anyway. So it was futile to want to see Nathan, to want to share anything with Nathan.

'Poppy? So what do you think? Shall I tell him yes or no?'

Huh? 'Petra, I am so sorry. I didn't hear any of that.'

Petra raised an eyebrow. 'I said I'm sorry if I've overstepped and I know your private life is none of my business, but Nathan is downstairs.'

'Nath… Nathan? My Nathan? I mean, not mine but…'

A ghost of a smile flitted across Petra's face. 'Nathan Larrimore,' she said. 'That Nathan. He asked if you'd see him. I said I didn't know. If you don't want to that's fine, I'll send him on his way.'

'I… I… No. It's fine. I'll see him.' She knew she had to, knew whatever he had to say she wanted to hear it, and if he, as she suspected, simply needed reassurance that she was OK, then she'd give it to him.

OK. Right. She could do this. But, oh, how she wished she'd known about this earlier, could have dressed for the occasion. As it was she was smart casual; she and Petra close enough now that there was no longer a need to show 'business Poppy' at every turn. So she was in simple flared black trousers and a cropped top, her hair tugged back into a ponytail. Her wedged shoes and her chunky statement necklace the only added pizzazz.

Not that it mattered.

'Right. OK. Well, I'll—'

'Just go, Poppy. Nathan's waiting outside. We'll catch up later. And…whatever is going on, I hope it works out how you want it to.'

'Thank you.'

Poppy walked down the stairs, her hands sweeping down the now familiar polished wooden balustrade, her heart beating so hard she could hear it. Somehow she kept her step measured, pulled the front door open carefully and there he was, standing next to his car on the opposite side of the road.

Nathan. The impact made her almost sway, but she forced herself to maintain her walk, concentrated fiercely on putting one foot in front of the other as he pushed off the car and came towards her.

'Nathan.'

'Poppy. Thank you for seeing me.'

She could see the tension in the rigidity of his shoulders, the clench of his jaw. But it was his eyes that mesmerised—they looked at her as though they were drinking her in, absorbing her image. And she was doing the same, wanted to brand his image on her brain, her eyes scouring him for signs of change. She was desperate to reach out to touch to make sure he was real.

'No problem. Though I am curious what you want to see me for. If it's to make sure I'm OK, I am fine. If it's because you're worried about the wedding—I won't be there. I mean, I'll be in Copenhagen on call, but I won't be a guest and I won't be there unless something goes wrong, which I'm sure it won't.'

She had to stop talking, but she couldn't seem to shut her voice down. Terrified that if she stopped talking, she would throw pride to the wind and throw herself into his arms, declaring her love. 'So feel free to bring a plus one.' She could only hope the words sounded sincere.

'I'm glad you're fine and I'll bear that in mind but neither of those reasons are why I'm here. Why I wanted to see you.'

'Oh.'

He turned to the car. 'Is it OK if we go somewhere else? I have the distinct impression Petra is watching from a window and any minute now Greg is going to drive up. It turns out everyone has a vested interest in us.'

Us. 'There is no "us",' Poppy said, wondered when he didn't respond to the comment. Instead he opened the car door for her, waited for her to get in, closed it and went round to the driver's side.

'I wasn't sure the best place to go and then I thought maybe we could go to the park. That way nobody sees us and nobody overhears us.'

'That's fine.' In truth she didn't care where they went as long as she was with him. Foolish, self-destructive even, but she didn't care. As he drove and she watched his profile, his hands on the steering wheel, the shape of his fingers, his wrists...desire returned with a force that made her catch her lips in her teeth to prevent the small gasp from escaping. Because this desire was worse, because now she knew exactly how those fingers felt, knew what joy his body could evoke.

And so it was a relief to get to the park, to feel the freshness of the breeze to cool her fevered thoughts.

'So what did you want to talk about?' The words were snappier than she'd intended but she was too hot and bothered now to care.

'I wanted to tell you the truth. Tell you what I should have told you that morning in Copenhagen. Instead of hiding behind some spurious tale of betrayal. So I want to tell you about my marriage to Alexis.' They'd reached the shade of a massive tree and in almost tacit consent they sat down under it. Every sense heightened. The tickle of the grass through the cotton of her trousers, the roughness of the bark at her back.

'OK.' Part of her wanted to hear this and a part of her didn't.

'Don't worry. I'll be brief. I've let you, let everyone, believe that my marriage to Alexis was idyllic, perfect, wonderful. But it wasn't.' He sighed now. 'But neither was it the terrible, torturous mess I've come to believe it was. Because after Alexis died I've seen everything through the lens of the diary she left behind.'

Poppy tensed beside him, couldn't help it. That diary—surely it had been wrong of Alexis to leave it behind, a legacy that she must have known would hurt Nathan, a man she had claimed to love or at least had loved once.

She heard the smile in his voice. 'It's OK, Poppy. I love how you fire up in my defence, but it's OK. I do understand why she did it. Because she needed me to see her truth, how she felt, and the problem was I don't think I ever saw her truth. Saw her as she really was. And I don't think she really saw me.

'We had this fantasy ideal of a marriage and once we got married we never really talked properly about how we felt. And maybe that was my fault. I didn't want to talk and I didn't want to listen. You see, I had an idea, I had a mission. My marriage was going to be perfect, because I was going to be the perfect husband. A man who didn't gamble, didn't lie and most of all a man who provided security for his wife. A home, a lifestyle and a bank balance.'

'That doesn't sound so bad,' she said gently.

'Maybe. But it was more than that. I also wanted to do it my way. My ideas, my company, and that isn't what Alexis wanted. She wanted me to stay in banking, rise up in the banking world, realise my ambitions like that. That was the husband she wanted. Not an inventor, a welder, a man who wandered around with his head in the clouds, who was at work the whole time whilst she was alone at home. And I wouldn't have children, not until I was sure my company was safe, not until I was sure I could provide without the smallest risk of the whole house of cards tumbling down.'

'But you thought you had time to have children, time to spend with Alexis. It is tragic that you didn't.'

'It is tragic that Alexis died when she did. And I was at fault, in that I clearly didn't see that she was unhappy.'

'But she was at fault too. Because she didn't tell you. And…' Poppy hesitated, tried to marshal her thoughts with sensitivity. 'And maybe she wasn't as unhappy as you think. Or maybe what made her unhappy was the knowledge of her illness, the realisation that she didn't in fact have the time that she deserved. And that diary—it was written whilst she was ill and when maybe she did have mixed feelings about the unfairness of it all. Because it is unfair. But I don't believe you were a bad husband and, believe me, there are plenty of bad men out there. You aren't one of them.' She looked him straight in the eye. 'You're a good man, Nathan, a man who tried his best.'

'I did try my best. It may not have been good enough, but I can now see that it wasn't all bad. And that is thanks to you.'

'Me?'

'Yes. Somehow you have given me perspective. Made me see that it was possible for my dad to love me and still do all the terrible things he did. Made me see that a relationship is about mutual support. When we were in Copenhagen we worked together—as a team. Talked, made sure the other person was getting what they needed. You encouraged me to take time out, go to the gym to brainstorm, you tried out vegan products.

'But it's not just mutual support—it's mutual responsibility. In my marriage I believed it was all on me and I think that meant that's what Alexis believed too. I thought my job was to make her happy and she thought that too. It was the foundation for our relationship and it wasn't strong enough.

'I don't know what would have happened, if we would have worked it out, rebuilt on new foundations, or if we would have drifted further apart, and I can never know that. I don't regret marrying Alexis and I can see now that there were happy times and happy memories.' He paused. 'I went to the graveyard yesterday. It sounds mad but I talked to her and I made my peace.'

'I'm glad.'

'I needed to do that before I could see you, tell you all the truth, tell you what is in my heart.'

And now her heart did a little hop, skip and a jump as he turned to her and what she saw in his eyes shot a surge of hope through her, a shot of happiness that she struggled to dispel. Told herself you couldn't read anything into one expression.

'What? What is in your heart?'

'You,' he said simply. 'You and my love for you. A true love, a love that makes me happy and joyful. I needed to tell you about Alexis so that you could know that this love—I don't feel it is a betrayal in any way. When Alexis was alive I was faithful to her and I never once thought of you in an inappropriate way. Maybe Alexis could see something that I couldn't, but I did no wrong. And when you and I met again now, the woman I fell in love with is the Poppy Winchester of today, the Poppy who walked into my office and changed my life. But that love is not wrong, or a betrayal. It is a thing to be celebrated.'

He moved closer to her now. 'And please… I don't expect you to reciprocate, though God knows I hope with every fibre of my being that one day you will.'

'Stop. Nathan. There is no one day about it. I love you. Right here and now. I don't know how it happened, but it did. I love you heart, body and soul. Those days in Copenhagen you gave me so much. Belief in myself. On so many levels, professional and personal. You made me feel seen and understood. You changed my life. For the better. And I love you.'

She could see joy in his face, in the wide beam of his smile. 'You love me?'

'Yup. With all my heart, you're the person I want to be with. I love you.'

'And I love you. I cannot imagine ever loving anyone more. I want to wake up with you every morning. I want to share your dreams and share mine with you. I want to help and support you through whatever life throws at us.'

'I want us to balance each other and listen to each other, to laugh and cry together, to dance, walk, run and move forward with each other.'

'And do you know what is most important and what I know will happen? We are going to be happy together, happier than you can possibly imagine.' He rose and pulled her up, picked her up and twirled her round. 'And I promise you, Poppy. I will always see you. Always be there for you.'

And she knew he would.

EPILOGUE

Ten months later

NATHAN OPENED HIS eyes and, as it still did every morning, a sense of almost dizzying contentment crept over him at the sensation of Poppy's presence. Today she had slept snuggled up to him with glorious abandon, her body sprawled over his, her hair tickling his nose.

He stayed still, not wanting to wake her, knowing she must be exhausted after the previous day. Petra and Greg's wedding, the culmination of all her work, the hours spent making sure every detail was in place and the days and nights spent on the dress. The result had been all he had known it would be—spectacular.

And now today they had the day to themselves in Copenhagen and he felt a thrill of anticipation. This was the day they should have had months ago and this time he'd get it right.

She opened her eyes and her lips curved up into a smile.

'Good morning. Provided it is still morning.'

'It's still morning, and Copenhagen awaits,' he said. 'Only this time we can do whatever we want to do. And first of all we are going to drink a toast to the world's most successful wedding-planner-cum-fashion-princess.'

He climbed out of bed, grinned when she gave a wolf whistle. He tugged on his dressing gown. 'Right, give me ten minutes.'

In the designated time he returned with a tray. 'Smoked salmon, rye bread and a small glass of champagne. You drank nothing yesterday and I think a toast is in order. To Poppy Winchester.'

'I couldn't have done it without you. And I completely appreciate all your patience and support the last months.'

'Right back at you.' Because however busy she'd been, she'd found time to support him as well. To help him track down his father and, though they had yet to meet, they had started a conversation and, in time, maybe they would meet up. Poppy had also helped him prepare for the launch of the new company. And somehow they had also found time for each other.

Poppy grinned. 'At the risk of sounding im-modest, it was pretty good—Petra hugged me at the end and said she couldn't have imagined a better day. And they looked so incredibly happy, didn't they?'

'I don't think there was a dry eye when they said their vows. And the dress was stunning—if that doesn't launch you, I don't know what will.'

They clinked glasses and Nathan could feel bubbles of happiness fizz inside him as if in synchronised movement with the bubbles of the champagne.

An hour later Poppy glanced up at Nathan as they walked through the bustling streets of Copenhagen, sensed that he was brimming with anticipation, though she wasn't sure why.

'Where are we headed?'

'I thought we'd revisit the park,' he said, his voice over-casual, and her eyes narrowed.

'OK. Sounds good.'

Twenty minutes later they were walking along the grass and she gave a sudden smile. 'We're headed for where we had that infamous kiss.'

'Yup.'

As they approached the tree he slowed down, came to a stop. 'Well, what have we here?' he said in a tone of mock surprise.

Poppy saw the table, carefully laid under the sweeping branches of the tree. Snowy linen napkins, gleaming cutlery and a veritable feast spread out.

'And to begin with,' he said, with a flourish, 'oysters. And this time we can discuss their aph-rodisiacal qualities in as much detail as you wish.'

'How did you manage this?'

'Timing,' he said with a smile. 'And an at-tention to detail, learnt from you.'

'It's perfect.' Poppy sat down, blinked back a tear.

'No tears. In fact, because I knew you'd cry, I have a joke prepared to cheer you up. What's made of chocolate, has a shell and lives at the bottom of the sea?'

'I have no idea.'

'An oyster egg.'

Poppy couldn't help it—she gave a snort of laughter. And that set the tone for the next hour as they laughed and talked and ate and drank. Until finally he rose to his feet.

'There's one more thing.' And now his voice was serious, held something that made her heart race.

'Come over here.'

He led her a short distance away, behind a hedge, and she turned to him with a smile.

'It's a tandem bike.'

'Well spotted,' he said with a smile. And then he reached into his pocket, pulled out a ring box. 'Poppy Winchester. The last ten months have been the happiest of my life. Will you marry me? Move forward with me through life in tandem?'

And as she turned and looked up at him, she thought her heart would burst with happiness that this man, this wonderful man, who had provided her with the perfect proposal, personal and meaningful, wanted to marry her, just as much as she wanted to marry him.

'I will,' she said.

* * * * *

If you enjoyed this story, check out these other great reads from Nina Milne

Consequence of Their Dubai Night
Falling for His Stand-In Fiancée
Second Chance in Sri Lanka
The Secret Casseveti Baby

Available now!